Two Parts of a
SOUL

Two Parts of a SOUL

BY KATERYNA KEI

KEI INC
2019

Copyright © 2019 by Kateryna Kei

Cover design: RavenBorn

All characters and events in this publication, other than those clearly in the public domain, are fictitious and any resemblance to real persons, living or dead, is purely coincidental.

All rights reserved. This book or any portion thereof may not be reproduced or used in any manner whatsoever without the express written permission of the publisher except for the use of brief quotations in a book review or scholarly journal. No part of this publication may be otherwise circulated in any form of binding or cover other than that in which it is published and without a similar condition including this condition being imposed on the subsequent purchaser.

First published in 2013 by Kateryna Kei

ISBN: 979-10-91899-14-7

Ordering Information:

Special discounts are available on quantity purchases.
For details, please send an email to: contact@katerynakei.com

To Philippe, for all the inspiration that you have given me ;-)

Contents

The Baby 1
The Comeback 6
The Meeting 12
The Slave 22
Two Parts of a Soul 37
The Castle 42
The Hidden Room 52
Raven 63
The Nightmare 78
The Twins 84
The Star Gate 90
Randi 94
The Wedding Gift 100
The Ghost 109
The Blood Connection 116
Elena's request 124
Old Nim 135
When Strength Becomes Weakness 143
Epilogue 152
Acknowledgements 155

Kateryna Kei

THE BABY

Within the depths of the forest, Old Nim knelt in the middle of a clearing. Tall, untamed plants and flowers grew randomly around her, nearly obscuring her from view. This place was her garden, though it didn't look much like one. Old Nim didn't look like a gardener, for that matter. She was small and thin. Her hair was long and naturally golden, and her wrinkled face was lit by a warm inner light. Her smiling, sky-blue eyes were still beautiful, reflecting both calmness and a childish curiosity about the world. Kneeling there among the tall herbs, the woman looked like some sort of fairy or a fantastic illusion.

It was one of those sweet summer evenings when the air is filled with the aroma of flowering heather and the relaxing hum of bumblebees, the type where the sunset pours its honey over the grass and the trees, drawing their long shadows across the ground.

That particularly placid evening, Old Nim was gathering the herbs; her long, thin fingers ran along every plant, carefully studying each leaf and stem and sensing the smallest details, which no ordinary person would notice. She selected only what she needed, leaving no trace of her collection and remaining in harmony with nature.

Suddenly, her hand froze over the leaf she was about to touch. A barely perceptible trembling of the ground under her knees told her that someone was approaching. No sound was audible yet, but years of experience had made her absolutely unparalleled in reading nature. She remained motionless for a while, her eyes closed, as if taking a quick reprieve, and then she calmly resumed her work.

Meanwhile, the noise sounded, first as a distant humming and then as a clear, alarming clatter of hooves. A moment later, a foaming horse frantically halted at the edge of the forest, right before the clearing. The rider was a young woman. She dismounted and ran toward Old Nim. Her beautiful face was covered with dust, and her long dark hair fell loose on her shoulders, spilling over her ornate gown. Reaching Old Nim, the woman hastily fell to her knees.

"Nim," she called, panting, "help me!"

For the first time, Nim turned to face her, and her sky-blue eyes widened with concern and surprise when she saw the woman's gown was torn and stained with blood.

"It's a nightmare!" sobbed the young woman. She covered her face with her left hand, her right arm holding tight to a bundle.

Old Nim stood up and gently hugged the woman, patting her shoulder. "There, there," she said quietly, "calm down, for emotions blur your mind ..."

The woman abided, yet it took her some time to fully regain her composure. Finally, she stopped sobbing and straightened her back.

Nim waited in silence, her azure eyes shining with compassion and patience.

The young woman drew a deep breath and spoke, her voice quiet and strangely distant, as if she was in some sort of trance. "Father died right after midnight. Po wants me to marry him. He is talking about love, but I am sure he just wants to become king. I refused—it would have made no difference anyway for me, or for my people. Po then organized the rebellion against me—" she stopped, and her vacant glance widened with horror. "So many people died! It was ... It was ... I never imagined they could be so cruel to their own brothers and neighbors!" She closed her eyes, and her free hand formed a fist, as if in overwhelming agony. She growled painfully, like a fatally wounded animal.

Nim didn't let her dwell on the pain. "And your husband?"

The question had the effect of a slap to the face: the young woman straightened and looked at Nim, her glance alive and full of strength and fury.

"Po's got him, I'm sure of it! I saw it in his eyes. Po will do more than just kill him. That evil man wants to separate us forever ... Nim, I have to do something!"

In front of the raging cauldron of emotions that was this young woman, Old Nim remained serene and undisturbed. She had lived long enough to learn how to remain calm in any situation. Still, her voice was firm and serious. "How can I help you?"

The young woman had been expecting these words with such anticipation that when they finally came, she found it hard to gather her thoughts. She swallowed and held out her bundle to Nim.

"I managed to save Anna ..." Carefully unfolding a sheet, she lovingly caressed the tiny face of a baby. "My daughter ... the living proof of our love ..." she murmured with pride and affection before raising her eyes to Nim again. "Nim, I want you to take care of her."

Nim didn't say a word, and her face showed no new emotion, so the young woman went on. "I know I'm asking a lot, but you are our only chance! What Ronen is facing is worse than death. I must try and save him." Tears filled her eyes and spilled again, falling on the baby's cheek. She hurriedly wiped her face with her sleeve, but the baby woke up and smiled.

The mother bent and kissed the baby's forehead. "Anna, I love you," she whispered. "And your father loves you. Very, very much." She kissed the baby again and then spoke to Nim, never taking her eyes off her daughter. "Nim, you are the only person I trust enough to care for her. If I do not return, she will be safe with you. I want her to grow up pure and honest, like a true daughter of her family, like a true granddaughter of her glorious grandfather!"

Nim stared thoughtfully into the young woman's face for a while. After several pensive moments, she slowly nodded and held her arms to the baby.

"I've never had a child of my own and am honored by your trust. Melaina, I promise you, I will do any and all things necessary to protect her."

The young woman tried to smile, her lips trembling with emotion. Blinking rapidly to chase away the tears, she mournfully stated, "Thank you, Nim. I will never forget it."

They remained silent for some time as both looked intently at the baby, who was watching them with interest. Melaina bent down to kiss her daughter for the last time and carefully gave the baby to Nim. Wiping away her tears, she stood up and hurried toward the horse, which was waiting right where she had left it.

When she got in her saddle, Nim called to her. "Melaina …"

She looked back.

"You are the best magician I know. Stay calm, and listen to what your heart tells you. Gods help you!"

A sad smile washed over Melaina's face. She waved in a final goodbye, forever engraving in her memory the picture of the old woman kneeling in the middle of tall heather bushes and holding her only beloved daughter in her arms.

When Melaina was gone, Old Nim didn't linger. Quickly finishing her gathering, she put all the plants into a simple linen bag, then carefully hid all traces of human presence in the clearing. Her exit was as seamless and stealthy as her arrival.

Moving noiselessly and quickly for an old woman, she left no visible trace in her wake. The forest was her home, her element. She had been living there for ages, and no one was able to find or catch her there.

Soon she arrived at her hut, which was disguised with branches and plants. There she stopped to give the baby some fresh milk and to gather her most important possessions, which she fixed on her horse's back.

At nightfall, the small fellowship started their long journey east. It looked unusual and somewhat surreal: a small, fairylike woman, with her fair hair shining in the moonlight, a baby in her arms, and a horse and cow walking close behind her.

Nim was leaving. She didn't know whether she would ever come back, but she had given her word to Melaina. She was determined to protect the child by any means, even if she had to bear the pain of leaving home for the second time in her life.

THE COMEBACK

Anna grew up with Nim in the middle of a vast, dense forest. The fairy woman taught her how to talk to animals and plants, cast spells, make potions, and survive. At the same time, the girl had a truly royal education: she could sing, dance, play the flute, read, and write, and she learned good manners as well as the hierarchy of her people's society.

She looked more and more like her mother every day, with the exception of the color of her eyes: sky-blue, like her father's.

Nim taught her about the world through stories and tales, and she told her all that she knew about her parents.

When Anna was ten, Nim decided that it was time for them to go back, to try to find out what had happened after they left, as well as to have a glimpse of the present situation.

The girl was happy to travel and asked a lot of questions along the way.

"Aren't you tired of talking?" sighed Nim in a parental tone.

Anna rolled her eyes. "How can one get tired of talking? It takes so little effort—you are only moving your mouth! Tell me more about the sea! What are the good spirits living there like?"

Nim kept answering for a while longer but then concluded by stating, "Now it's my turn to ask questions. Tell me, which plants are you going to gather at full moon?"

Anna moaned with disappointment but answered, "Mistletoe, wild rose, lily of the valley, sea buckthorn, melissa, three-part beggarticks, inula, bearberry, and ledum."

"Aye, and also thyme. Don't forget it."

Before Nim could say anything else, Anna asked, "If you are making potions at black-moon night, are they going to affect the soul?"

"Not necessarily."

"But you said black-moon nights are for dark magic!"

"Aye, but dark magic does not deal only with souls."

"But you said the worst thing that can ever be done to someone is touching their soul!"

"Aye. If you kill the body, the soul is still alive, while if you harm the soul, you harm that person's existence in the Universe."

"It means that the person will not be able to live another life?"

Nim sighed and was visibly annoyed by this point in time. "Possibly. I don't know. But not all dark magicians are that evil. And, most importantly, very few of them are powerful enough for such spells. It's a very advanced and dangerous magic, one with a lot of power behind it. You should be aware of it, but make sure you have no other solution before trying it."

Anna thought for a while and went on with new energy. "Is Po evil enough? Does he deal with souls?"

Nim didn't answer right away. She thoughtfully studied her small hands and frowned slightly. "I cannot tell for sure. I haven't seen Po for many years now. He may have acquired that secret knowledge, for he used to experiment with complex dark spells and rituals."

She looked up and met Anna's curious gaze. "This is another reason for us to be very careful and alert. I don't want you to be scared or to panic, but remember that the less attention you attract, the better it will be for us."

Anna nodded. She remained silent for some time, but soon her questions resumed their merciless rate.

"Can a soul be destroyed?"

"Aye, in theory. But as far as I know, no human has ever done it. Generally, dark magicians would simply try to gain control over a soul or to imprison it somehow."

"Can you do it to a living person?"

"When you take control over a soul, the person must be alive, otherwise it's useless. It allows you to make the person act according to your will, generally in the name of doing some terrible things. You can recognize the affected people by the very drastic change in their behavior and by looking into their eyes—their pupils are always dilated, for their soul remains in the dark."

"And if you imprison a soul?"

"To imprison a soul, you must kill the person and catch the soul at the moment it is leaving the body. Then you have to put it somewhere and to surround it with spells that will hold it there. But it is very hard to do because a soul is not a physical object."

"And is there a way to get free of it?"

"Hardly, if the dark magician knows what he or she is doing. But then again, I don't know for sure. It's another reason for you to remember your protective spells, young lady. Come on, recite …"

Anna heaved a sigh. "All right, you win again … First there is …"

By sunset, they had arrived at Nim's previous home. It stood there as before, only now branches and tall wild herbs hid it completely, as if the hut had grown into the tree, becoming an integral part of the plants themselves.

Nim and Anna dismounted and walked carefully toward the hut. They looked like sisters playing an exciting game: the same height, the same dresses, waist-length free-flowing hair, and a similar slender shape. But while Nim's hair was bright golden, Anna's was black, and Nim's thin face was covered with lines, a reminder of the several hundreds of years that she had lived on Earth. Anna examined the place with obvious excitement and admiration, while Nim looked alert and tense, like a wild animal coming to the river.

They silently approached the hut from behind and made their way into the stable, where there was a hidden door leading into the hut. Anna didn't notice it, so when Nim suddenly pulled it open, she gasped in amazement.

Nim ordered the girl to remain in the stable then she carefully stepped into the hut and started examining it. She had an outstanding memory and knew exactly where she had left everything.

To her surprise, it looked like no one had been there after her sudden departure. There was no trace of Melaina, or of any other intruder.

Prudent as she was, Nim checked the hut for any spells or traces of magic, just in case, but it was clean.

"May I come in?" Anna begged impatiently.

"You may now," Nim allowed, and the girl hurried inside.

The hut was very simple. It had two small windows, now completely hidden by wild plants, and just one room that served as kitchen, dorm, and living room all at the same time. There was a small fireplace and minimal furniture. The place was covered with layers of dust, but Anna loved it instantly.

"Where can I make myself a bed?" she asked, her voice eager.

Nim, who was busy smelling the potions that had remained there during all those years, looked at her with studied irritation. "Don't you think we ought to clean the place first?"

Anna shrugged innocently. "I wasn't intending to go to bed right now …"

The next morning, Nim took Anna to the sea, which she had never seen before. When they got to the rocky coast, Anna froze, speechless. Blue waves rolled toward the land from the very edge of the horizon to hit the rocks and fall down as white foam. Seagulls flew over the sparkling water, and their screams echoed around them. Anna took a deep breath, filling her lungs with salty air.

"Come, there is a beach down there," called Nim. "We'll swim."

Together, Nim and Anna swam and played in the water until Anna's lips turned blue with cold. Afterward, they lay on the sand, sunbathing. Nim showed Anna some edible mollusks and algae and explained how to eat them.

In the afternoon, they went to the clearing where Nim had last seen Anna's mother. The clearing looked just as it had before—randomly growing tufts of heather, their sweet-smelling pink flowers attracting insects and bumblebees.

Anna walked the path over and over, trying to imagine her mother doing it, trying to feel her thoughts and emotions at that moment.

"Do you have any idea what could have happened to them?" she asked finally.

Nim gave her a quick glance from behind a bunch of

flowers that she was gathering. "Well, that's what I'm intending to find out here. There is no doubt—Melaina never came back here, or to my hut, after that day."

Anna's eyes sparkled with hope. "What can I do to help you?"

Nim didn't answer straight away. She carefully lowered her flowers on the grass then stood up and walked toward the girl. She put her hands on Anna's shoulders and met her gaze. "Anna, I'm sorry," she said quietly. "None of them are alive. I do not pretend to be the best magician, but I can surely feel when people dear to me die, and I felt Melaina dying. I don't know exactly what happened that day, or whether or not she was able to save your father. All I know is that she died willingly, and it may be important for us to know why."

Tears filled Anna's eyes. "Why didn't I feel that?"

"You certainly felt it! You started crying, and I was unable to calm you for quite a while. But you were too small to remember it."

The girl swallowed and looked away. "Do you think I need to become the queen?" she asked after a while.

"I wouldn't advise you to undertake that. At least not yet."

THE MEETING

Once a week, the town celebrated market day. Foreigners, travelers, and all sorts of traders arrived from a myriad of directions at dawn, and throughout the whole day, they sold or traded their goods in the streets of the town. This day was considered a holiday; it was a good opportunity for townsfolk to wear new clothes, to meet new people, and to simply entertain themselves.

That May morning, the sky was cloudless and blue, birds sang happily, and the gentle breeze carried the intoxicating smell of flourishing trees. Warm weather reanimated the trade, and the market was even more crowded than usual.

The most prestigious and expensive merchant rows were hidden from the sun under a removable roof made of tied pine tree branches. That place was the most crowded of all the rows, with acrobats, illusionists, and even gapers.

A tall bald man walked among the colorful crowd. He wore a long white silk tunic and matching cloak with golden embroidery. Several rings with differently shaped precious stones shone on his long fingers, and one large golden ring with engraved symbols circled his bald head. His face was pale and perfectly shaven, and he exuded a strong sense of power. His thin face, with an aquiline nose and beautifully shaped violet eyes, could have been considered handsome if not for his constant scowling expression and pursed lips. It was Po, the main priest and real ruler of the country.

That day, Po was in his usual bad mood, which his servants had come to consider the norm. The kingdom was gradually falling into a crisis, even though Queen Elena was completely under his control, yet it had nothing to do with his bad temper. The kingdom and its situation did not bother him much at all. Po made sure he would survive and keep all his wealth, no matter what. The people around him were too common and primitive to serve for anything but his magical experiments. All of them had weaknesses, and Po was so good at finding and using these weaknesses, that he was beginning to find it all becoming boring.

People feared the main priest. Po was well known for his cruelty and constant bad mood, but no one talked about it out of fear. Everyone knew that Po was a very skilled magician. Apart from him and his priests, no one was allowed to perform magic of any kind. All the magicians had been killed or banished from the town, and the use of magic of any kind was officially prohibited.

However, magic was the only thing that still interested Po, and he eagerly and greedily gathered secret knowledge from everywhere. Thus, he was coming to the market to keep an eye on people and at the same time to see whether foreign traders had something interesting for use in his magical studies.

Two guards and a slave boy accompanied him, not that Po really needed guards; his magical knowledge was more than sufficient to protect him from any possible attack. He was only using them to intimidate the townspeople as well as to show his importance and high social stature. On the other hand, the guards were useful when the main priest had to publicly do something dirty, like punishing some scum.

Po's slave boy was small, disproportionate, and even somewhat girlish. He was obviously from the north, for his skin was pale and his hair was very blond. He was seven, but ill fed and bony as he was, he looked younger. There was something animalistic in his furtive, lurking glance and in his bent shoulders. He looked as if he was always expecting a kick. The boy was barefoot, and his rough oversized tunic made his bony body, with its long arms and legs, look grotesque. Moreover, his colorless eyes shone with hate, only increasing the unpleasant impression he was producing.

Po held his slave on a large silver chain, which ended with a ring that was constantly locked around the boy's neck. When he was angry, or just wanted to punish the boy, he pulled on the chain, causing his victim immense suffering.

The guards escorting Po were total opposites of the slave boy. Both of them were very tall and muscled. Taller and wider than the main priest himself, they were obviously well fed and cared for, and they appeared to be relaxed, looking around with lazy indifference. They knew that their appearance alone, with menacing swords on the hip and glittering metallic armbands around their colossal forearms, dissuaded any attempt to get closer to the procession.

Po walked slowly among the foreign traders. Organization was definitely missing within the market: nuts, spices, and fruits were sold right next to furs, jewels, stones, and dishes. Po deeply disapproved of it, but he knew from experience that it was the best place to purchase interesting things. There were even a couple of traders from whom he consistently bought items.

One of them, a small, fat man with a ponytail and quick, cunning eyes, spotted the priest from afar. A greedy sparkle lit his small eyes and made his lips part in a cheesy smile. All the traders knew that Po was a real moneybag, and if there was something, even a useless little thing that caught his attention, the price never bothered him.

Po stopped in front of the fat man and coldly answered his greetings.

"Do you still have that crystal cup you brought last time?" asked the priest.

The trader's heart sank. "Your Highness, unfortunately, someone bought it from me last month." He was genuinely sorry to have to disappoint his best customer. "But I've got something special to show you—"

"Who bought it?" Po cut him short, without paying even a speck of attention to his sales pitch.

The man's eyes rolled as he tried to recall the details. "It was a lady traveler. She was moving east with her new husband and wanted the cup for her jewels," he answered finally.

Po nodded. No emotion showed on his face, but he felt satisfied.

Taking it as a good sign anyway, the trader resumed his strategy. "I want to show you something, Your Highness …" he started conspiringly. "I got my hands on it by pure chance and thought of you just as I saw it …" He hurriedly dived under his counter and started searching his boxes.

"Of course, you don't have to buy it," Po heard his muffled voice. "But as this object is unique and extremely rare, I think you should see it."

He emerged from under the counter red-faced and panting, he was simply not in good enough shape for such endeavors. His eyes shone, and his fat, short-fingered hand held a small leather parcel. Carefully unfolding the parcel, he displayed its contents to the priest.

Po remained impassive, yet even before he saw the item that was inside, he knew he had to have it. What he saw surpassed his wildest expectations: he was holding a palm-sized, perfectly round blood-red ruby. Just as the daylight touched it, the ruby started shining with a mysterious red light. The stone looked alive, as if it had its own powerful and capricious personality. It seemed as if it was observing the people around it, reading their deepest thoughts and fears.

Po watched the ruby, speechless. He was more than fascinated.

"It is called the 'Dragon's Eye,'" the trader whispered mysteriously. "It's a unique gem from a big island far in the south. People say it has a very strong character and can even kill ..."

While Po was admiring the red stone, his guards grew bored, waiting for their master. Yawning lazily, they looked around at the women passing by. The slave boy, taking advantage of everybody's lack of attention, slowly started moving toward the neighboring counter, where a couple of noisy women were buying fruits. Big and juicy white peaches were lying there and calling to him. The boy had never tasted one before, but the sweet smell emanating from them was so appealing, and his stomach had been empty since the previous morning. Unable to resist the temptation, he decided to steal one of those beautiful fruits, or at least to die trying, for his life was tough and worthless anyway.

Trying to look casual and to not attract attention, he slowly moved toward the peaches, which formed a tidy pyramid at the edge of the counter. Blankly staring at the ground, he felt more aware of the world around him than ever, observing the people around him with every cell of his body.

It seemed to him that a lot of time passed until he finally got to the wooden counter where the fruits were laid. There, he dared lift up his head and looked around.

The two women were arguing loudly with the trader about the price, and Po and his guards were not watching.

Moving very smoothly, he reached out and seized the closest peach.

Again, no one seemed to notice. A wave of pleasurable

anticipation swept over him. As he pulled the fruit toward him, however, the whole pyramid moved slightly.

Petrified, the child froze. The thought of what would happen to him if the whole pile fell down sent a cold shiver throughout his spine. Irritated by the sweet smell, his stomach started rumbling even louder, and the desire to taste the beautiful fruit was so overwhelming that, shaking with fear, he held out his free hand and grabbed an orange from the bag of one of the arguing women. Then, quickly removing the peach, he stuffed the orange in its place.

The peach pyramid shivered slightly but did not fall.

Sneaking the stolen peach under his tunic, the boy slowly moved back, struggling to keep his knees from shaking, and hid himself behind Po. Only then did he finally dare to breathe.

Meanwhile, the fat trader was triumphantly closing the sale; Po was obviously very interested. His eyes were fixed on the stone, and his nostrils flared nervously. He bent forward toward the trader, catching every single word.

"See, there is a round emptiness right in the middle of the stone. An air bubble, I guess. Its color is always slightly different. It makes the stone look like a living eye that watches you. This species is absolutely unique, and it needs a master whose power can overpower its own, otherwise—"

"How much?" interrupted Po, his voice calm and firm again.

"Fifteen metrctcs of gold," answered the trader, and instantly regretted it. It was nearly ten times the price he had paid for the stone, and it was too much, even for a man as rich as the main priest.

The latter slowly looked at the trader. His pupils were narrow, and it was impossible to read anything in his cold violet stare. He stared unblinkingly at the trader for several eternal heartbeats, and the fat man's anxiety skyrocketed. He cursed his consuming greed, nearly sure that he had just lost his best client.

Suddenly, the priest spoke.

"I'll give you two metretes right now, and I'll keep the stone. As for the rest of the gold, my servants will bring it to you by sunset."

The trader's heart leaped happily in his chest. He had trouble suppressing a huge sigh of relief. He rubbed his hands together, discovering that they were sweaty, which was appropriate, considering how frightened he had been.

"Deal, Your Highness. Anyway, I was not intending to leave before tomorrow."

Po wasn't really listening. Carefully covering the stone with leather, he hid the parcel safely in his pocket and was intending to pay as agreed, when a shriek made him jump.

"You, you little thief!"

Po swiveled on his heels and quickly assessed the situation. It was a woman who had shrieked, and the trader from the closest counter was now yelling with her, angrily pointing in Po's direction.

"He stole my fruit!"

Fruits were the very last thing Po was interested in, so he instantly understood what might have happened. Without even looking back, he jerked the silver chain fixed around his forearm.

Petrified by the screams and panic, and blinded by a sudden and violent pain, the slave boy fell on the ground, coughing and fighting for air. The half-eaten peach fell from his juice-covered hand and rolled in the dust.

Po slowly turned around to watch the boy suffering. He pulled violently on the chain again and again. Wheezing and wriggling in the dust, his helpless victim was in agony, nearly asphyxiated. The boy's face went red. The metallic ring cut deep into his skin, and fresh blood ran on the collar of his tunic. He cried as dust covered his face and filled his mouth and nostrils.

The guards watched the boy's agony in amusement, leaning lazily against the large wooden columns that supported the roof.

The crowd of onlookers formed a circle around the priest and his prey, some of them petrified, while others became excited at the sight of blood and suffering.

The main priest kept pulling on the chain, again and again. His violet eyes shone with immense satisfaction in his cold, stone-like face. Absolutely deaf to the child's pain, he seemed unable to get enough of the mere sight of suffering.

Suddenly, a tiny figure jumped out of the crowd and seized the silver chain, shouting, "Stop it!"

The crowd gasped at the daring of this skinny, dark-haired girl.

Po froze, taken by surprise.

Quick as a flash, the girl knelt by the slave and touched the ring at his neck. Maybe the lock couldn't stand the repeated harsh pulling, or maybe there was some other reason entirely, but the ring sprang open, releasing the boy.

Still coughing and swallowing for air, the slave clung to her arm as if it was a source of life, receiving the healing energy she was sending him.

Meanwhile, Po was back to his senses. He was given a new, fresh victim to punish! His thin lips twisted in anticipation of the new pain. Slowly savoring the moment, he raised his free arm, ready to cast a spell upon the girl.

As if she felt his intention, the girl looked up at him, and their eyes met.

The priest's eyes widened. He suddenly felt breathless. All

the blood left his face, and he instantly forgot the spell he was about to use.

It could not be true. It was unbelievable! It was her! Hers was the face that had been haunting him for so many years! A flow of memories washed over Po, fresh and painful, as if it had happened only yesterday. A beautiful young witch with unknown ancient magic. She had to belong to him! He had been plotting everything for years, through suffering and humiliation, and he had been so close to his aim, so close! But she left him with the bitter, consuming anger of defeat and with burning, unsatisfied desires. She was the source of his dearest aspirations and deepest pain. He thought he would never see her again, but miraculously, here she was!

The girl wasn't disturbed by his reaction. Awarding the priest a disdainful glance, she said angrily, "Shame on you! He's just a boy! It's so easy to hurt someone too weak to fight back!" Then she looked down at the boy, who was still panting, his head now lying on her knee.

Po remained silent. He needed to calm down. He took a deep breath to slow down his madly racing heart. "Would you prefer me to hurt someone stronger?"

The girl blinked in disbelief. "I don't want you to hurt anyone at all!"

Po couldn't take his eyes off her. He still couldn't believe it was not an illusion. He would keep her. She belonged to him. It was logical. She was his reward for so many years of suffering. Struggling to regain control over his swirling thoughts, and scrambling to think of some spell to use, he asked, "What's your name?"

The girl flashed him a dirty look, intending to respond, but Po never heard her response. With a deafening crack, a wooden column supporting the roof broke under the back of one of the guards.

The man yelled with pain and fear, falling backward. The crowd shrieked, drowning all the other noises. Instinctively, the guard tried to stop himself, seizing the edge of the fruit counter, and it crashed too, covering the man with a hopping and rolling avalanche of fruits and vegetables.

For some time, panic seized the crowd. Screaming in fear, people moved chaotically away from the crash. However, the roof didn't fall completely; only one of its edges hung low above the stands. Little by little, the panic stopped.

Standing among the dusty fruits, Po stared at the broken chain on the ground. Both the girl and the slave were gone. Anger and disappointment washed over him, making him snarl like a wounded animal. "Where is she?" he yelled at the other guard. The latter could only shrug helplessly.

"Find her!" he barked as he threw the chain on the ground. He did not need it any longer.

"Watch me, Melaina," he muttered to himself. "Who will win now that you're back?"

THE SLAVE

Meanwhile, Anna ran down the closest street. The boy was clinging to her hand. Despite his weakness, he was doing his best to keep pace with her, for he knew that his life depended on it.

However, he soon slowed down, and a fit of coughing shook his frail body.

Anna stopped and looked around with exasperation. They were in the middle of a tiny empty street. Stone walls ran on both sides, separating them from yards and houses.

She was not going to leave him now. "We must climb," she announced, and he only nodded.

A large ceramic vase stood by the wall. Anna lifted up its wooden cover and instantly let it fall back with a grimace of disgust—it was filled with stinky slop.

They had to hurry. Anna placed her feet in the gaps between the stones of the wall and climbed, stepping carefully on the wooden lid of the vase. It was thick enough to bear her weight, but the vase was shaky. Quick and agile, the girl heaved herself on top of the wall and glanced around.

A yard and a house. An old stable was a bit farther away. The place looked empty.

Anna turned and beckoned to the boy.

It was harder than she had expected. He was weak and still panting. His body shook, and his bare feet slid on the wall.

Anna tried hard not to hurry him, but her instincts

screamed in alarm, and her nerves were ablaze. She knew the guards were already looking for them. From the top of the wall, she spotted a piece of rope on the ground.

"I'll be right back," she whispered to the boy and jumped from the wall into the yard.

The wall was quite high, and the ground below was dry. The shock sent jolts of pain through Anna's legs, but she instantly forgot about it upon hearing the sound of their pursuers. Panic seized her insides, making her heart pound in her ears. She had to save the boy. Nim had saved both of them by breaking that column, and now it was up to her. She seized the rope and climbed back.

The boy was still on the ground. His feet were bloody, and tears of fear and exasperation ran down his dirty cheeks. Anna's heart ached at the sight of him. Cutting the approaching noise of running feet away from her mind, she threw the rope down to the boy and managed an encouraging smile.

He caught the rope with a new hope and started climbing. He was smaller than Anna, yet heavy enough that she had to pull on the rope with all her might to keep it from sliding down.

The pursuers were nearly there, and Anna could no longer control her stress. "Quickly, quickly," she urged him in a whisper.

That was a mistake; the boy's eyes widened with panic, and he lost his foothold. He nearly fell, but his foot found the vase, which began to sway dangerously.

Reacting quickly, Anna extended her hand out to him. He reached up and grasped it as the vase lost its balance and fell, spilling its stinking contents all over the street. At that moment, the pursuers appeared from around the corner.

"Catch them!" Po's guard shouted, but no one was particularly eager to step into the downstream of slop.

The guard's voice frightened the boy. He started climbing again. Breathless, Anna seized him by the tunic and pulled with all her weight, her knees pushing into the wall.

It worked. They half slid, half fell down into the yard. Anna heard the boy groan with pain, but she did not stop. They were not safe yet. She pulled him to his feet, and they rushed to the old stable.

The stable was empty. The stale air smelled of dust and rotten straw. Sunlight was only visible through the holes in the old roof.

Anna led the way to the attic, and barricaded the entrance with old straw and pieces of rotten wood. She was almost done when the sound of footsteps and voices told them that their pursuers were in the yard.

The children froze in fear, straining their ears and not daring to breathe.

Someone broke into the house and was rummaging there while others searched the yard.

Suddenly, the old door of the building squealed and opened. The boy shivered and bit his lip. Drops of sweat appeared on his forehead and temples.

Several men came in.

Anna's heart was pounding in her ears. She bit her fits to make her breathing less audible.

The men's voices seemed too loud. They searched the place, carelessly kicking pieces of old junk that littered the floor.

The children were silently jumping at every kick. The boy closed his eyes and was crying hard. If they were found, the consequences would be dire.

Po's guard stormed into the barn. The mere sound of his voices made the boy shake violently. Anna gave him a terrified glance. But he didn't seem to be able to stop it. His teeth started chattering with fear. A cold drop of sweat ran down Anna's spine. The men were going to hear them! She had to do something.

She noiselessly moved to the edge of their barricade, her heart madly racing. Through a hole between the pieces of wood, she saw the man standing right next to the shaky wooden ladder leading to the attic. Under Anna's petrified gaze, he started climbing. The old wood cracked under the man's weight. This time, there was no escape.

The patch of light coming through a hole in the old roof fell upon him. An idea popped into Anna's mind, and in a moment of fervent inspiration, she looked up and noiselessly uttered a spell.

A rotten beam above squealed and cracked. Slowly at first, then faster and faster, it fell down, bringing with it a rainfall of straw and dust.

The men yelped and hurriedly jumped from the ladder, avoiding the beam by mere inches.

Anna was too scared to take chances; another beam was already falling down.

Bending low and covering their heads with their arms, the men hurried away, leaving the door ajar.

A happy smirk lit Anna's face. Relief washed over her. She took several deep breaths to calm down her racing heart. Her hands were shaking. After some time, she turned toward the boy. He was gaping at her in fear and disbelief.

"What?" she asked in a whisper.

He blinked and swallowed before finding the use of his voice. "You're a witch?"

It was the first time she'd heard him speak.

"Aye," she shrugged.

"Witches were banished from this town!"

"Really? But Po, the main priest, still does magic!"

"He's the only one allowed ..."

Anna eyed him attentively. "Why was he torturing you, anyway?"

The boy shrank. His expression turned fearful and hunted again. "I stole a sweet fruit," he babbled.

Anna was horrified. "You mean, he does that to you often?"

Without looking at her, the child just nodded.

Anna frowned, revolted. Nim had told her that Po was mad, cruel, and dangerous, but somehow she'd had trouble imagining it until now.

Gradually, the voices outside died away. Their pursuers were gone. Anna carefully removed their barricade and stepped on the ladder. "Stay here and keep quiet," she told the boy. "I'll find us some water and food, if we're lucky."

She returned quickly. Their pursuers had left the house door ajar, and she found a loaf of bread and some water there.

While the boy ate, she carefully washed his feet and, with the use of a couple of spells, healed every single scratch on them.

Greedily biting into his bread, the boy watched her attentively and then asked, "Can anyone become a magician?"

"Dunno ... I guess. You must learn it."

The boy's eyes sparkled, but he kept chewing his bread, clutching it with both hands as if someone was about to take it from him.

"Can you teach me?" he whispered, his expression both pleading and excited.

"Well, it takes a very long time ..." Honestly speaking, she didn't feel like explaining magic to him at that very moment. She felt tired because of their running and climbing; stress and magic only adding to the exhaustion.

The boy began to beg, watery tears slowly rolling down his tired face. "Please … please, one spell! Only one spell!"

The girl heaved a sigh. After all he had been through, she couldn't bring herself to say no to him.

"All right. Stop chewing and help me to take care of your neck, and then I'll explain to you the spell I just did."

The boy beamed. The smile almost made him look attractive. Reluctantly, he put down the rest of his bread and straightened his neck.

Anna healed it and started explaining the spell to him, but he didn't want to learn the healing one; how to break the beam seemed much more useful and exciting to him. Finally, Anna quickly explained to him how it was done and then stretched out on the wooden attic floor.

"Magic always drains your energy, so don't practice too much," she yawned and added, "I'll have some sleep, and you should as well."

When the sun set, Nim noiselessly appeared in the stable.

Both children were fast asleep, curled side by side on the attic floor.

The boy felt her presence first. He woke up and eyed her with bleary vision. Then he quickly recoiled, pulling Anna's hand to wake her up.

Anna opened her eyes and yawned. "What?" Then she saw Nim and smiled. "It's Nim. She won't harm you."

Anna sat, rubbing her eyes, and the boy crouched close by her side, hiding from the fairy woman, whom he obviously still mistrusted.

Completely undisturbed by the boy's doubts, Nim opened her bag and pulled out some bread, cheese, and a flask of milk. She quickly divided it all between the children.

They took the food and started chewing energetically.

The woman waited patiently then produced out of her bag several juicy apples.

The boy eyed her with deep gratitude and even gave her a weak smile, eating all the while. She had obviously won over his trust.

"What's your name?" Nim finally asked him, and Anna turned to look at him as well.

"Slave"

"What?" Anna gasped. "It can't be!"

He looked at her, confused, but then he shrugged. "Well, they also call me 'filth' or 'ugly.' Whatever."

"That's horrible!"

The boy stopped chewing and thought for a while. Anna's words troubled him.

"Do you remember your parents?" Nim asked.

The child nodded with conviction. "They are strong and beautiful, with dark hair and suntanned skin." He met Nim's piercing blue gaze and went on. "One day, they will come and save me from the priests and their guards ..." The more he talked, the more his conviction faded. "They will ... love me ..." he trailed off in a whisper, bitter tears filling his eyes.

Anna passed her arm around his shoulders and stroked his untidy fair hair.

"It's all right," she whispered. "I have no parents either."

The boy started crying. Anna threw Nim an inquiring glance, silently asking her whether there was something they could do to help him.

Nim only nodded. "Give me your hand, and I'll tell you about your parents."

Making sure Anna was still hugging him, he obediently held out his dirty palm to the fairy woman.

She looked at it for a while and then slowly said, "Your mother is alive, indeed. After you were born, your parents took a boat to go to another northern land. They took you and your brothers with them, but the ship was attacked. Your father died, and you and your eldest brother were taken. Your mother and your unborn second brother reached the land they were heading to. They grieved most heavily your loss and the loss of your father and brother."

The boy stopped crying. He was listening eagerly, catching Nim's every word.

"Can I find them?"

Nim smiled and nodded. "Of course. It all depends on you. You are free now. You only have to make sure the priests never catch you again."

The boy frowned. A lot of different thoughts crossed his mind. Finally, he asked, "But where will I find them, and how can I recognize them? What if they never accept me?"

"Oh, they surely will!" Anna reassured him. "I bet you look exactly like them. They are tall, with fair hair and pale skin, they are strong and brave, and ... they must have the same shape of face as you."

The boy wiped his nose with his tunic and touched his face. A shimmer of new hope was shining in his eyes.

"I think it will be easier for you to find your brother first," Nim told him. "He is a slave in the town by the eastern sea. We can take you there, if you want. Your brother is older than you. He works with the fishermen. He looks like you. His real name means 'eagle' in his native tongue."

"What's my real name?" the boy asked eagerly.

Nim frowned. "I don't see it clearly. It has no particular meaning ... your mother came up with it, I guess."

The boy's shoulders sank. "I don't want to be 'slave' anymore."

Anna's face brightened. "Nim, you are the best magician and the wisest person in the world. You can give him a nice strong name!"

Both Nim and the boy blinked. None of them had thought of that.

The boy reacted first. Straightening his back and finally leaving Anna's arms, he caught Nim's hand and begged, "Please, give me a name!"

Nim bit her lip. She hesitated for a moment while the boy watched her. Finally, she smiled.

"All right, then. I'll call you Alan, which means 'fair' and 'handsome.'"

The boy considered it for a while, bemused, and then asked, "'Fair' ... because of my hair?"

Nim smiled again. "Because of your hair, too."

The boy waited for her to explain further, but she said no more. As for Anna, she was beaming.

"I like it," Alan said finally. "Thank you."

Nim only nodded.

Some time later, the three of them left the stable.

The night was warm but cloudy. The rain was approaching, and no stars were to be seen. It perfectly suited their small group; none of them wanted to be seen. They moved silently and warily. Nim walked first, and the children followed her, holding hands. Anna was sincerely worried for Alan and his ability to stay silent in the dark and not hurt himself, but the boy was doing really well. His hard life as Po's slave had taught him a lot of useful survival techniques—being small and unnoticed among the most important. He had no trouble moving noiselessly and skillfully avoiding holes and objects.

They didn't speak until they got to Nim's hut. Once there, Nim showed Alan where to wash himself and managed to find him some clothes, and then she returned to the hut with Anna.

"Thank you for saving us," Anna told her.

Without looking at her, the woman answered, "Anytime."

There was an edge of stiffness in her voice that made Anna feel guilty.

"Nim, what's wrong? Are you mad at me?"

Nim turned to face her. "Nay, I'm not mad at you. As for the wrong, after you so splendidly introduced yourself to your worst enemy, I think we will leave before the sunrise! Po's guards have been looking for you all day long! They searched all the houses in the town!"

Anna rolled her eyes. "All day …? Did they really?"

"Aye. You look very much like your mother. Po recognized you instantly. Didn't you see how he looked at you?"

"Not really. How?"

Nim tilted her head, recalling Po's expressions. It was rather hard to describe.

"I'd say surprise, satisfaction, evil interest. Maybe even a bit of thirst for revenge. He didn't expect to see you but obviously decided that you were a much better prey. This is the reason why he let you help his slave out, and the reason why we are leaving."

"Oh …" Anna slowly realized the danger Nim's smart spell had saved her from. Who knew what would have happened if Po had managed to catch her? Her intuition told her that nothing positive would have come of it. And now, their chance to find out what happened to her parents was surely ruined. Suddenly feeling miserable, Anna asked, "Do you think I shouldn't have intervened?"

"I think it was dangerous and foolhardy," replied Nim,

making her heart sink. "But I don't blame you, for I know I would have done the same."

Anna scratched the tip of her nose, hiding a smirk. She knew she was the luckiest person in the world, for she had Nim by her side.

They left when it was still dark. They rode in sleepy silence until breakfast, at which point they began talking.

Alan told them about his life at Po's, including the various cruelties and habits of the main priest.

Nim occasionally asked him some questions, and Anna listened attentively as well.

The more the boy talked, the more relieved she felt that she'd saved him.

In the evening, they stopped and made a fire. Alan happily participated in the cooking process, eagerly listening to Nim's explanations about edible roots and plants.

"You may need this information one day, now that you are free," Nim told him.

Alan chewed on his lip. "I can't wait to meet my brother. But what if he doesn't like me?"

Anna smiled encouragingly, "Of course he will! He must be just as eager to find someone from his family as you are! Anyway, you'd better expect it to turn out fine. If it turns out badly—which it wouldn't, I'm sure—you will have enough time to worry."

Alan thought for a while and then grinned. "I'll try." He watched Anna cut plants into pieces and throw them into the kettle. He added, "I'm sorry that your parents left you."

Anna nearly dropped her knife. "Oh, nay! They did not leave me! They are dead."

Alan muttered another "I'm sorry," and the conversation moved to a different subject.

That night, Anna couldn't sleep. Alan's words kept turning in her mind. No matter how hard she tried, she could not get rid of them. The truth was that she could not find enough arguments to deny it. It sounded too true; her parents had left her, after all. The more she tried to turn away that thought, the more it hurt. Lying in the dark, she tossed and turned, unable to find rest.

"Anna," Nim's quiet whisper nearly made her jump. "Why don't you come and talk when you feel upset?"

The girl didn't know what to say. She couldn't put her finger on the real reason why.

Nim already knew what was wrong. "They only left you because there was no other choice."

Anna felt bitter tears filling her eyes. Nim said it too: they left her! The pain of this realization was almost too much to bear. Anna felt miserable and small and very lonely. She pressed her fist to her mouth and cried silently, her body shaking.

Nim reached out to caress Anna's hair with her warm hand.

For some reason, this gesture provoked a new feeling in Anna: anger. A strong, consuming anger against all of them—her parents, for leaving her and making her hurt, for Nim for not telling her, for … everything! Pushing Nim's hand away, Anna snapped, "She could have stayed!"

"Nay, she couldn't!" Nim's words fell like a blow. Anna had never heard that tone before. It made her shiver and stare at the old woman. "That's very selfish of you to think so! You would have wanted your mom to suffer? Tell me!"

Anna swallowed, lost for words.

Nim went on in a calmer tone of voice. "Your parents shared a soul—I have already told you this. If your mother had run away with you, crazy priests would have done unspeakable harm to your father. If they managed to separate your parents completely, both Ronen and Melaina would have suffered immensely. Forever, or until it was undone. You don't understand, not yet, but one day you will. You will meet the other part of your soul too, so try not to judge until you fully comprehend the situation."

Anna felt confused. She tried to wrap her mind around what Nim had just told her.

After some time, Nim added, "Your parents did not fear death, but they were facing worse than that. How would you feel if you had to watch your mother suffer, day after day, knowing that it is because she chose to stay with you instead of saving her beloved? How would you feel, knowing that in order for her to be with you and watch you grow up, your father had given up everything—his very soul?"

Anna was speechless. Silent tears ran down her face, but the anger was gone. She did not understand it completely, but she knew Nim was right. She felt sorry for her selfish thoughts.

Nim reached out and hugged her. Anna hugged her back, crying even harder. Nim held her until she calmed down, caressing her hair. Then she helped Anna to get into her makeshift bed and adjusted her blanket.

"I'm sorry," Anna muttered guiltily.

Nim smiled down at her. "It's all right. Everyone makes mistakes." She bent down and kissed the girl's forehead. "Sometimes, you have to let go of someone you love. It does not mean that you cannot keep them forever in your heart and mind."

Several days later, they reached the town where, according to Nim, Alan's brother lived.

Nim and Alan went looking for him, while Anna had to stay in the forest in case Po's people were still looking for her.

Anna hated waiting. She tried to occupy herself as much as she could: she gathered enough mushrooms and berries to last for at least three days, swam in the river, listened to the birds and animals. During this time, however, her thoughts were with Nim and Alan, and she kept returning to the clearing where they had to meet.

Nim returned alone when night fell.

"We found his brother. He is a good boy. Alan is with him now," she said.

For some reason, Anna felt a bit sad upon hearing this news. Alan seemed to her so small and unprotected. She couldn't help thinking they should have kept him with them.

Nim easily guessed her thoughts.

"It's better for him this way. He's got his own life, and it does not go the same path as ours."

Anna gave her a doubtful glance. "But what if he gets caught, or what if somebody else enslaves him? He's not used to living on his own. And how will he find food?"

Nim just grinned. "Don't worry. His brother will look after him, and Alan is stronger than you think. One day, he will be stronger than you."

Anna's brows raised in surprise. "What did you see?" she asked eagerly.

Nim didn't avert her glance but shrugged. "I didn't look too far into things, but I saw that you are going to meet him again, and he will somehow help you out."

Anna bit her lip. She itched to know it all, but Nim only looked into the future when there was an urgent need for it, and this wasn't that kind of situation.

"All right, then," she said finally. "At least I can be sure that he will survive."

"He definitely will," was Nim's answer.

Two Parts of a Soul

Ten years later

Anna rode to the town alone.

The morning was pleasantly warm and bright, the sky was crystal clear, and birds sang as if it were spring, giving a joyful pallor to the day.

Anna wore a simple brown travel gown, just like most of the women in the region. Her long dark hair fell loose on her shoulders and back, only maintained by a leather strap across the forehead. A nearly empty travel bag was attached to her saddle, next to the flask of water. She had left her bow in their forest hut, trying to seem as ordinary as possible. She was relying entirely on her magical skills in case of danger.

Ten years had passed since their last visit to her native town, and the events that had occurred during all this time only stimulated Anna's already burning curiosity.

They had arrived a week ago, yet Nim didn't allow her to go into town out of consideration for her safety.

This day, though, was special. When she'd woken at dawn, Anna knew she could not stay in the forest any longer. The urge to go to town was stronger than ever before. She had waited for Nim to leave and then snuck out of the hut, hiding her trail to make it look as innocent as possible, at least for some time. She thought that a little ride would do no harm. She only wanted to look around, and she was driven by the desire to find out something about her parents.

She rode to a hill from which the whole town was visible and stopped there, watching.

To her amazement, the town seemed empty. The streets were unusually clean; houses stood silent and were decorated with flowers. The white walls of the castle reflected the sun, throwing light onto the closest buildings, but even the castle seemed empty.

There was something attractive and cozy about this town that she barely knew. In its motionless silence, the town displayed traces of her ancestors, of their wisdom, and of the artisanal skills they used to build it. Unable to resist the temptation, Anna hurried her horse down the hill and slowed, exploring the empty streets and fully enjoying that feeling of wonder and freedom.

The last time she was there, the town was rather dirty, and instead of flowers, the streets were covered in litter and slop. Here and there the poor begged for some bread or money, but today, it looked stunningly glorious and beautiful. Curious by nature, Anna decided to find out what had happened and led her horse to the beach. It lay lower than the rest of the town, at the foot of the last hills. As she approached, she heard the sound of music.

The town had no port. The coastline was too rocky, and the beaches were too small. This particular beach was the largest. It had two long wooden moorings where various fishermen's boats were docked.

Slowing her horse, Anna mounted the hill on her right to have a good look without getting too close.

What she saw caught her by surprise. Nearly all the inhabitants of the town were there, gathered alongside the road and on the closest hills. The queen, the priests, and their guards were lined on the beach, wearing their best robes.

On their left, a group of musicians played happy tunes.

But it was not the crowd that caught Anna's attention; the most beautiful ship she had ever seen stood at anchor in front of them. A Viking ship. Its dragon-headed bow was delicately curved, and so was its stern. It was light and gracious, and Anna could bet it was very fast. The ship's sail was lowered, but a white flag with the insignia of a bird was flying on top of the mast. Mostly fair-haired sailors sat on oars and waited for several local boats to approach.

Soon, the local boats were back with several sailors and gifts for the queen. The sailors from the beautiful ship stepped on the dry land. They were tall, bearded, and strong. One of them, apparently their captain, stepped forward and raised his arm to greet the crowd.

Drastically contrasting the traditions of their hosts, whose social ranking was visible via their clothing, all the sailors were dressed equally. Just like his people, the captain wore a simple white shirt under a thick leather jacket, leather trousers, and boots coming up to the knee. The only thing that set him apart was a big black raven perched on his shoulder.

The crowd started answering his greeting, but the queen and the priests remained motionless and disdainful, doubtlessly waiting for a more elaborate salutation, and thus alluding to their leading position. The cheerful roar died, suffocated.

Anna knew the man understood it, even though he didn't show it. She froze, eagerly watching the scene from her observation post.

The captain lowered his arm and looked at the queen. He stopped walking and just stood there, his back straight and his feet slightly apart, as if he were still on the moving deck of the ship.

A piercing croak of his bird suddenly echoed through the beach.

It was so loud and unexpected that it made most of the people jump. The music stopped, suspended in midair, and the cheerfulness instantly gave way to uneasy tension.

This was only the beginning. The raven seemed determined to get a more pronounced reaction. It spread its powerful black wings and rose into the air. With a rapid and menacing manner, it flew toward the crowd.

A collective gasp of fear rent the air. People hurried to duck down or move out of the way of the terrifying bird. The queen bent over and covered her head with her arms. Even the priests' expressions were no longer disdainful.

But the raven didn't touch anyone. It flew over the crowd and up the hill toward Anna, followed by the panic-stricken stares of several hundreds of eyes.

Anna's horse neighed in fear and stepped back. Anna instantly steadied the mare with her knees. She held out her arm, calm and proud, her eyes on the bird.

As if accepting her invitation, the raven suddenly landed on her wrist. It folded its wings and tilted its head slightly, watching Anna with seemingly intelligent eyes. Anna stared back, curious.

From the raven, her glance traveled to its master. The man was looking at her.

It felt as if a flash of lightning ran through her. Suddenly, Anna was breathless. The man's emerald-green eyes were looking straight into her soul, dazing her. She shivered, and her lips parted in a silent gasp as she felt a powerful rush of energy bursting out of her chest. It stretched toward the man, suddenly forming a strong invisible bond between them.

Everything changed. It was as if a missing piece of her was finally put in place, and she had become what she was always meant to be. The whole universe felt different around her.

It was *him*. She knew him with all her being; she had known him forever, long before she was born. It was so simple and so true. Anna's heart swelled in her chest, and tears filled her eyes. She had been missing him; she had been living for him. Every single step and breath she had taken were leading her to him. He was her true love; he was the man the prophecy was talking about. The very core of her whole life. The other part of her soul.

He knew it as well. Taken aback, he raised his brow slightly.

Anna was unable to take her eyes off of his, to break that magical connection, even though her instincts screamed in alarm. The raven on her wrist suddenly took off and flew back to the man.

As if waking up, Anna saw all the heads turned toward her. Among them, another pair of eyes caught her attention and made the hairs on the back of her neck stand up. Violet and ice-cold, the eyes of the main priest reminded her of a poisonous snake, ready to strike.

Terrified, Anna turned her horse, and it galloped down the hill, away from the beach.

Two Parts of a Soul

THE CASTLE

Leaving was painful. Anna's heart hammered in her ears, and her cheeks felt hot. Her very being burned to get back to him, as if she were pulling on the invisible bond between them. The more it stretched, the more panicked and lost she began to feel. A dull, throbbing pain was born inside her, light enough to stand without wincing, but disturbing enough that she could not ignore it. The man stood out vividly in her mind. She knew his strong, suntanned shoulders and the silk of his long, fair hair. She knew the sweet tenderness of his lips and his smile, which seemed to illuminate everything around him. It felt like remembering something dear and long forgotten, and with every step her horse made, the urge to get back to him grew inside of her.

With a mixture of panic and overwhelming happiness, she realized that from now on, it would always be so; she would never feel right without him near. All of her existence had suddenly changed, completely and forever, and despite the pain and unease of being away from him, she felt thrilled, moved, nervous, and something else that she could not find the word for.

Anna pressed her hands to her temples, desperately trying to regain at least some control over herself while her horse galloped on her own in the streets of the empty town.

Only when the mare suddenly came to a halt did Anna return back to reality. She blinked, staring at the carved wooden doors of the castle. They stood unprotected, with not a soul in sight.

Anna's thoughts swirled around with a rapacious speed, taking a different direction. Though she was unable to completely forget about the man she had just met, she was at least able to think about something else. She had come to the town to find out about her parents. However, her impulsive intervention on the beach had been most likely interpreted as an offense to the queen. In addition, Po, her worst enemy, had seen her—so much for staying unnoticed! Nim would surely be upset when she found out. Anna wasn't intending to lie to the fairy woman, and she felt bad for making Nim feel upset. She had to go back to the forest. Immediately.

The unprotected castle door in front of her made her hesitate. What if this was her chance to learn something? Looking back on her misdeeds for the day, Anna concluded that adding another one wouldn't make any difference, so she dismounted.

The castle, shaped like a huge seven-edged star, was silent and inviting. The smooth, white marble of its walls shone brightly in the sunlight. It looked magnificent and mighty. Anna knew its story, of course.

Built a very long time ago by the first king of this land, the castle stood in the same condition as when it was first constructed, symbolizing the greatness of their ancestors. It was well known all over the country, from one sea to another, and maybe even farther.

Ages ago, the first king married a foreign princess, and came to this land with her. They needed a fortress to protect them from any enemy, so they built a unique castle. The princess was from the south, and her wish was to keep the sun in her home forever. For that, the king found the best craftsmen, and they worked the finest white marble into the walls to make it shine like a precious stone, change colors with the sun, and glow in the dark. No one ever found the secret of that incredible ancient technique, but the princess got what she wanted; the castle could keep and generate light. An unassailable fortress from the outside, it had a long balcony running on top of it. It was said to be very warm and cozy inside.

Anna stared in awe. Just to think that she was born there! So many secrets were hidden behind those beautiful, shining walls. The sense of mystery and anticipation tickled her insides. Glancing around to make sure she was still alone, she pushed the wooden door.

It was locked. Anna grinned. She was a witch. She always had her magical sign with her for such occasions. Figuring out how the door was locked, she reached for the bracelet where her sign hung. Both her wrists were decorated with at least a dozen bracelets, each serving a different purpose. She knew each of them by touch, which was useful in times like these.

However, it was not there. Surprised, Anna looked down. The bracelet was gone. She checked her pockets and shook her skirt. Nothing. Then it suddenly occurred to her what had happened; the raven had sat on her wrist! It must have stolen the bracelet. How amazing! The raven took the most useful bracelet of all, as if it actually knew what it was!

The mere thought of the raven made Anna's heart accelerate madly, drowning her in an avalanche of invigorating feelings and memories. She had to lean her head against the cold marble and slowly count to fifty-seven before she managed to regain control over her swirling thoughts. No matter how pleasant those thoughts and feelings were, she had to tune them out. She was on her enemy's territory and already in trouble. Therefore, she needed her head clear and her senses sharp.

Her magical sign would have been of much use, but she could still do magic without it. She pressed her hand to the door and muttered a spell. The heavy wooden bar moved and fell down on the other side. Anna pushed the door and slid inside. She carefully locked it behind her and turned to face her past.

She was in a high stone passageway, which led to the yard. Alert for any sign of movement, she silently walked to the end and peered out of the corner.

The yard was clean and empty. Stables ran from the entrance, ten on each side. Their wooden doors, with rounded tops, were polished by thousands of hands.

Anna stepped into the yard and looked around. Just to imagine, her parents and grandparents had lived here and ruled over their people! She was the first of the whole family who had grown up outside. Bittersweet emotions swept over her. What would it have been like to grow up here, surrounded by her family? How great would it have been! It was the life she was born to live, the home and happiness that had been unfairly taken from her. As there was no one to disturb her, her imagination conjured up figures from the past, revealing to her the familiar and long-hidden traces of her family.

The doors to the front donjons were located right after the stables. From Nim, Anna knew that in the right donjon were the kitchen and the stock premises, while the servants lived in the left one.

She couldn't help smiling as she noticed the covered stone bridge, supported by solid round columns that linked the donjons to each other from outside, forming a high gallery. How exciting it would have been to play hide-and-seek there! Every object around her felt like her old friend, as if everything was greeting her after a long absence. As if a hidden door opened in her mind, she suddenly discovered that deep inside, she was already familiar with this place. She had always known it. Eager to investigate further, she walked to the kitchen door.

It was locked. Guided by her instinct, Anna bent down and slid her hand over the old bricks of the wall. In a tiny hole, right above the old bucket, she found a large key. She took it out and inserted it into the lock. Her heart fluttering, she watched the door open.

She knew what was on the other side before she actually saw it: two stone stairs leading to the large high room, with a fireplace and a huge oven on the left, shelves with dishes on the right, and two fountains in the center.

The kitchen looked exactly as she knew it would. It was lit by a single torch, and numerous dishes and plates filled with the freshly-cooked festive meal stood ready on the long tables. It smelled so good that Anna's stomach started rumbling. However, she didn't touch a thing. She stepped outside, closed the door behind her, and bent down to put the key back to its place.

That was when she sensed it: someone or something was standing behind her. Anna immediately spun around, and froze, staring into the beetle-like eyes of a large gray hound.

The dog smelled the air, distrustfully examining her, and then moved aside, as if trying to circle her. It was a big shabby mongrel, and it looked quite dangerous.

A thought flashed in Anna's mind: what if the priests have trained the dog with magic to guard the castle? The dog could easily inform Po of any intruder. She could not allow that to happen. Staring at the animal, Anna slowly stretched her hand toward it, ready to cast a spell.

The dog smelled the air again and suddenly swayed its shabby tail, welcoming her.

Anna froze in place, unsure.

The dog carefully stepped closer and sniffed her gown. It didn't look threatening anymore.

Anna offered him her open palm as a sign that she meant no harm, and the dog's cold, wet nose touched it. Then the dog turned around and trotted away. It stopped under the stone bridge and looked back at her, its head slightly tilted to the side, inviting her to follow.

And Anna followed.

A beautiful garden lay behind the stone bridge. A white stone alley led to the fourth, central donjon. In the middle of the alley was a large white marble fountain in the form of seven dolphins. The dolphins stood on their tails, each facing a different donjon and spitting large jets of sparkling water into the blue pool. A cloud of multicolored bright drops floated into the air around them.

Anna watched this with awe. It was at least nine feet high, and the dolphins seemed to be smiling at her. White stone alleys led to other royal donjons, two on each side. The air by the fountain was fresh and delicious, and the cloud of drops enveloped Anna as she approached. Smiling, she held out her hand and touched the water. Next to her, the dog drank from the pool, snorted loudly, and trotted to the second alley on the left. Anna followed the dog again.

This alley was smaller than the main one and was surrounded by trees. The flower carpet disappeared, replaced by some tidy green grass. Anna spotted a small and elegant wooden arbor hidden behind the trees. It looked so cozy and charming that she was tempted to come closer. She suddenly thought of the green-eyed captain. The arbor seemed to be the right place for a date with him.

The dog's impatient bark pulled her out of her fantasies; the animal ran to the right, across the grass, and disappeared behind the flowering bushes.

Anna hurried after the dog and came to a small clearing. There was another small fountain there. It was sculpted in the form of two dolphins facing each other, their beaks and tails nearly touching. Water fell out of their smiling beaks and from under their dorsal fins, making them look like a heart, surrounded by glittering jets. In Anna's opinion, it was definitely the most beautiful place in the world.

The dog sat on its hind legs.

Anna approached the fountain and leaned on the stone edge of the pool, listening to the whispers of the falling water. She slid her hand into the water, enjoying the coolness on her skin. The gentle, caressing sound of water slowly filled all her being, wiping away the thoughts and leaving her in peace and harmony with nature. She let it be; Nim taught her that every place held secrets and traces of people who had been there before, and only by being very attentive and opening all of her senses could she perceive it.

Her reflection trembled slightly on the greenish surface of the pool. Anna watched it without concentrating on the details. Time stopped, and it felt very pleasant. A yellow leaf slowly fell into the pool, making the greenish surface shiver. When the little waves disappeared, Anna noticed another reflection opposite her. The reflection was barely visible. A strikingly familiar beautiful woman with sad eyes watched her from the opposite side of the pool. The hairs stood up on the back of her neck. Anna could see that no one was really there, and she stopped breathing, trying not to blink so as not to chase away the vision. The woman was smiling, her eyes feasting on Anna.

"Mother?" Anna whispered, overwhelmed with emotions.

The smile on the faint face widened, and Anna's eyes swam with tears. She blinked.

The greenish water was still shivering, but only Anna's

reflection was visible on the trembling surface. The vision was gone.

Anna jumped to her feet and hurried to the place where it had been. No one was there. No trace, nothing! Only her own crying face was reflected in the place where she had just seen her mother. Desperate to find out more, Anna glanced around and spotted a wooden donjon door. She walked to it and pushed it open.

She found herself in a large circular room with a big wooden table and several fine chairs. Different cult-related objects stood on the small stone tables by the walls. It was the fifth tower, and it was obviously occupied by the priests. Driven by her burning curiosity, Anna briefly inspected the room and the objects but found nothing interesting, apart from a skillfully hidden large staircase leading upward. She went up and found herself on a long balcony overlooking the garden. A dozen doors ran alongside it. Anna carefully opened them, one after another, only to discover those were the priests' dorms. Each of them contained multiple beds and simple wooden furniture.

Of course, Po's room wasn't there. Anna found it two floors above; an impressive wooden door with complicated carvings protected the room that occupied the entire floor. Anna's first thought was to try and get in, but then she accidentally discovered a small, well-hidden staircase at the opposite end of the corridor. She wouldn't have noticed it if it weren't for a bright-red butterfly that flew into the corridor and suddenly disappeared on that wall. Intrigued, Anna came closer and saw the butterfly sitting on a wooden step of the hidden staircase. Someone of amazing talent had created the wall painting that, combined with the natural light and shadows, made the small staircase invisible to the eye of everyone who was not standing right in front of it.

Anna examined the small staircase eagerly. It seemed there was a solid wall at the end of it, but it could have been another perfectly crafted illusion. Nim loved to say that the most important hidden things were right under one's nose. After some deliberation, Anna decided to go upstairs first.

She checked the staircase for any protective spell but found none.

She made it halfway up the staircase when she heard the dog barking outside. Her heart raced in alarm—it was a warning. The greeting ceremony on the beach was over, and everyone was back to the castle. She was trapped.

In one stride, Anna got to the top of the staircase and whispered a spell that would open a lock. Nothing happened. Anna's panic skyrocketed. She glanced back in exasperation, already knowing that it was too late for going back. The sound of approaching voices reached her, making her knees go weak. Her breathing was coming out quick and rasping. Now she really felt the foolishness and irresponsibility of her actions.

A door opened somewhere below and several people came in. Biting her lip, Anna assessed the situation. She was completely exposed here, standing on the wooden staircase. She had to move. She looked at the solid wall in front of her and tried hard to think clearly.

The voices were getting closer—someone was coming upstairs.

Anna tried the opening spell once again, and when it gave no results, she went on with a spell to remove protection, and then to remove a magical seal. The wall emitted a spark of light that hissed and vanished. It worked! Relief flooded her whole being as Anna performed another door opening spell, pushed the hidden door open, and slid in.

Her hands shaking, she locked the door behind her and finally dared to exhale. She was safe!

The only thing that she completely forgot was to remove any spell that would warn whoever sealed the door of an intruder. Enjoying the feeling of relief, however, Anna was far from thinking about it.

Two Parts of a Soul

The hidden room was dark with dusty stale air. When Anna's eyes got used to the darkness, she spotted a window hidden behind a pair of black heavy curtains. Carefully avoiding the silhouetted objects around her, she walked toward it. She pressed her hand over her nose and pulled on the curtain. The daylight streamed in through the impressive cloud of dust that instantly enveloped the young woman. Moving away, Anna bumped into what appeared to be a massive wooden table covered with old books and rolls of parchment. She steadied herself and turned to look around.

She guessed the room used to be an office or a library; wooden shelves ran alongside most of the walls. There were two chests of drawers and several chairs, also covered with rolls of parchment.

Anna decided to examine the table first. A large, leather-covered book on top was a register. Careful, beautiful writings that could have belonged to her grandfather, or his father, informed her about cattle and goods that the town possessed and sold in a particular month of a particular year, and about people who were born and who died every year. Taken by a sudden curiosity, Anna found the year her mother and father were born, and then looked all the way to the end of the book, hoping to see any notice of their deaths. But the register stopped the month of her birth, with many pages left empty.

After some thought, Anna returned to her mother's birth

and started moving backward, trying to find a record of Po's birth. Nim could read people's characters and destinies by their day of birth, and Anna thought this information might be useful to them. But even eighty years back, there was still nothing about the main priest.

Disappointed, she closed the register and briefly examined the rest of the mess. All the books and parchments were related to the external life and trade of the town. She would have found it interesting had the situation been different, but at the moment, she left it there.

She went around the table and even bent down to check its wooden legs for any possible hiding place, but there was nothing special about it. Why would Po bother sealing the door if there was nothing in the room? Straightening her back, the young intruder looked up and froze. Her blood turned cold, and her breathing caught in her throat—a full-size portrait of her mother stared unblinkingly at her from above a chest of drawers.

Melaina stood straight and proud, her head tilted graciously. Her dark hair was tied behind her, and a small, elegant diadem circled her forehead. She wore a sky-blue dress that suited her so well. The portrait must have been done by a master who knew the ancient secrets, for the woman seemed alive—even her eyes were glittering.

Anna's eyes feasted on her. She didn't even register how close she had gotten to the painting. It was the first time she was really seeing her mother, and afraid to even breathe, she tried to remember every single detail, to engrave it forever in her heart and mind.

The more she watched, the more it seemed to her that her mother was there with her, alive, breathing and feeling, and that she was silently communicating with her. Anna opened her heart, mentally telling the painting how much she loved and missed her; how every night she lay in her bed, watching the sky and imagining that somewhere in that eternal darkness her parents were two bright stars shining next to each other, forever united in their love. She loved thinking that they watched her from time to time, sending her their love and protection from far above. There were so many questions she wanted to ask, so many things she wanted to tell her, but instead, only strong, complicated feelings and emotions swirled inside her and flew toward the portrait. But deep inside, she was certain that her mother understood. It was a weird communication from a living heart to a painted one, and Anna could swear that tears appeared on her mother's eyes and a light smile touched her painted lips.

The sound of approaching footsteps abruptly pulled Anna back to reality. Someone was coming. The steps were slow but firm, slightly louder than normal. Whoever it was, they knew she was here, and they were savoring the chase, willing her to panic, knowing that there was no way for her to escape. It was exactly the way of the main priest. But how did he know?

Anna gasped in horror, there must have been a spell to warn him! Blind panic grew inside her as she glanced around helplessly. The first thing her eyes fell upon was the dusty gray window. In one silent movement, she got to it and hurriedly pulled back the curtain. The cloud of dust enveloped her again, only this time, Anna inhaled it in full. Unstoppable, horrible waves of coughing rose in her chest. She stopped breathing to suppress it. She could not make any noise!

A wooden stair squeaked slightly under Po's foot. He was very close. Too close.

Not breathing didn't help. The dust she had inhaled was irritating her throat, and her body was struggling to cough it out. Anna pressed her hand to her mouth and nose to muffle the sounds and fell to her knees, rolling into a ball under the table. It was a real torture: tears ran down her face, and her whole body shook violently in a desperate need to cough and to breathe.

Po was already behind the door. He would open it at any moment. She would be caught, and the nightmare would be over. A part of her willed him to catch her faster, so that she would finally be able to cough that dust out and breathe again, but then she heard someone running.

"Your Highness! Your Highness! Will you come, please?" called a muffled voice.

Anna was dying. Instead of the wooden floor, she could only see bright spots that danced around her with every convulsive shake of her body. Through that nightmare, she heard Po's voice uttering a curse and then a spell to seal the door so that she wouldn't get out.

Then he hurriedly went downstairs and away.

Anna's hand jerked, releasing her grip on her mouth against her conscious will. She filled her lungs with air, coughing and crying at the same time. It seemed to take forever. When it was finally over, she lay weak on the floor, panting in relief. Life felt incredibly sweet once it was over. Anna suddenly imagined how comical the whole thing must have looked from aside, and a hysterical laughter shook her. After all, she had always been the one to complicate things with something as stupid as a mouthful of dust.

Still giggling, she got back to her feet and shook the dust off of her dress. She then wiped her red face with her sleeves. It must have made it even dustier, but she didn't care. She was alive, and no one had caught her yet.

She tiptoed to the door and listened. Everything seemed quiet. She had been given some more time.

This time, careful not to breathe, she pulled the curtain

open again and returned to her mother's portrait. A chest of drawers stood under it. Anna didn't take chances and first broke any possible seals and protections around it.

The first drawer was filled with rolls of parchment. Most of them were about her mother's cousin, whose daughter, Queen Elena, now ruled over the kingdom. Anna found the official order proclaiming her rule and other related documents. All of them were covered in dust, and after a brief glance, Anna unceremoniously tossed them on the floor. She wasn't intending to take the throne from Elena, and it simply didn't interest her.

At the very bottom of the drawer, a surprise awaited her; the nearly last parchment was a portrait of her mother's family. Her grandparents stood smiling and happy, surrounded by their three children: her mother and the younger sister, and their little brother, who was at that time but a boy, brandishing his wooden sword with cute seriousness.

Anna looked at the portrait, her heart aching. They were her ideal of a perfect, loving family. Questions swirled in her head: What happened to her aunt and uncle? Did they really die of some illness, as it was officially stated? And what of her grandmother?

Unwillingly putting the portrait aside, Anna continued searching. She stuffed all the other parchments back into the drawer and opened the second one. It was also empty, as was the third one.

As she touched the fourth and final one, it emitted a sparkle, indicating that it had been magically protected. Smirking, Anna pulled it open. Inside, there was one carved wooden box. She was surprised to find there was no dust on it. Obviously, this was the core of the secret of the room, the hidden object.

Anna removed the box from the drawer and placed it on

the floor in front of her. It was not heavy, though it was quite large. When she opened it, she found it nearly empty. It contained two rolls of parchment, a long dark curl held by a silvery lace, a masculine ring, and a dagger.

Anna took the first roll of parchment and unfolded it.

Ronen, my love,

My heart is aching, for I cannot be by your side and hold your hand at this time. Anna and I, we both miss you very much.

Anna is such a wonderful baby! She is an avid listener. I am telling her stories and poems, and she listens in awe, her blue eyes wide. I wish you would sing to her—I want her to experience the magic of your voice.

I am so fortunate to have you! There are no words to describe how I feel about you. If it weren't for your love, I think I would have gone mad already. Something very bad is coming, Ronen. I can feel it, but I cannot stop it.

Father is dying. He is feeling worse every day. I have tried everything—medicine, potions, magic, spells ... but nothing works. I know Po is behind it, but he hides his game very well, and I cannot find any proof. I tried to talk to him, but it has been to no use, so I have forbidden him to come anywhere near Father. I personally make and bring Father food and water, and still he does not get any better. I am hurting with him, and I feel so helpless!

Please, be very careful, and don't trust anyone.

Love you forever,

Melaina

Anna sat quite still, holding the parchment in her hand. A mixture of joy and grief swept over her, making her eyes water again. Her mother had written it, her hand had traced these letters! And she wrote about her, Anna!

She reread the first paragraph, trying to picture it; her mother bending over her, smiling and telling her stories

Two Parts of a Soul

that, unfortunately, she was then too small to remember. Her father had a very beautiful voice ... Mother loved his singing ... Did he ever have a chance to sing to Anna, his only daughter? Perhaps not. Nim told her that during the last days of the king's life, Ronen's parents caught the fever. He went home as soon as he learned about it but was unable to help—they died one after another, and he buried them the day the king died. And then Po took the power and declared Melaina's wedding invalid. The priests caught Ronen before Melaina could get to him. Po promised to let Ronen live if Melaina would marry him, the main priest, and thus make him king.

Anna wanted to read the letter again and again, but she had to hurry. Po had sealed the door and could return at any moment.

She carefully put the letter into her pocket, together with the family portrait, and took the second parchment.

Ronen, my love,

I dreamt of my little brother, who came to me as a spirit. He told me that he, Mother, and Geenia were dead and that I had to run away as soon as possible.

I woke up to find that Father had died.

This is just the beginning.

Wait for me at nightfall by the Star Gate, and please, be very careful!

Love you forever,

Melaina

Anna's heart pounded in her chest as she relived this all over again with her mother. She knew they'd never met by the Star Gate. Did her father even get this letter? Most likely, he would have destroyed it as soon as he had read it, just as the previous one. The letters must have never reached their destination. Po had intercepted them.

Something else was written at the bottom of the second letter. Anna unfolded the parchment further to read it.

Unfamiliar, large handwriting with left-extended low strokes wrote:

Melaina,
Despite your betrayal and obstinacy, I cannot stop loving you. This is the proof of your divine predestination to me. You are the only woman great enough to be by my side, and I will never give up. I will correct your errors. For you and for me.
Blood will atone for your sins
The holy blade will pierce the sinner's heart
A soul will never reach the afterlife
You will be mine in this life, or I'll follow you into forever

A cold shiver ran down Anna's spine. Breathless, she stared at the parchment, shaking in her hand. The madman wanted to destroy her father's soul, to make him disappear forever. What if Po had done it? Nay, it couldn't be. Nim told her that Ronen and Melaina were whole and happy. Still, Anna felt butterflies in her stomach—they were also dead. Both of them. Her glance fell upon the dagger in the box, and goose bumps erupted over her arms and back. Was it the blade he had written about? Was it the dagger that killed her father?

Her mouth dry, and her breath caught in her throat, she slowly reached out. Her hand was trembling. She didn't want to touch it, but she had to if she wanted to learn something about her parents. Summoning all her courage, she closed her fingers around the dagger and took it from the drawer.

It was big enough to kill a man, and the silvery hilt was decorated with a ruby-eyed skull surrounded by magical signs. Her fingers numb and trembling, Anna slowly removed the leather scabbard and gasped. The blade was covered with old, rusted bloodstains. Anna felt her head spinning and nearly dropped the dagger. That was it. That was the dagger that claimed her father's life. Po hadn't even wiped the blood away, and he'd kept it hidden here. Anna saw in this another piece of proof that spoke to the perversity of this man, and she felt deep revulsion for Po. She hurried to put the dagger back into the scabbard. She wanted to find out what had really happened to her parents, but the dagger seemed too disgusting to carry in the pocket. Anna unceremoniously pulled a couple of the queen's documents from the first drawer and wrapped the dagger in them before stuffing it in her other pocket. At least she wouldn't touch it directly.

The long dark curl in the box obviously belonged to Melaina, and Anna put it with the letters and the family portrait.

The sudden sound of the approaching footsteps made her jump. She grabbed the box to stuff it back into the drawer, but something rolled loudly inside. Anna froze and opened the box, careful not to move it. The ring. She took it and hurriedly closed the box and the drawer. She would give it a proper look later.

The footsteps were approaching, just as merciless and even as the first time. There was something lifeless about them—like a clock counting heartbeats down to an irrevocable death.

Anna knew she had to get out. The only door was not an option, but there was still the old, dusty window.

Her thoughts became clear despite the growing fear as she closed the dusty curtain and dived behind it. A sudden inspiration made her use a spell to hide some of her traces—all the dust in the room instantly rose in the air and then slowly fell down, evenly covering every object and wiping out her footprints.

The window looked as if no one had touched it for at least twenty years. Anna cast a clever spell and climbed out.

The footsteps stopped behind the door. She had to hurry.

Swallowing down her fear, Anna stepped onto the tiny decorative cornice and closed the window behind her. The ground was too far below, and her footing was shaky, but there was no other way around. All her senses sharpened by fear, she heard the door opening. She started moving alongside the cornice as fast as her gown and her tense muscles would allow. Should Po have decided to open the window, he would have spotted her instantly.

Anna forced herself to breathe and move, trying not to look down.

A massive stone drain ran down the wall, and Anna slid into it, hitting her knee, as she pressed herself to its slippery green walls.

She didn't have time to adjust her hold or her footing when the window squeaked open. Anna stopped breathing, pushing her hands and knees into the slimy walls of the drain with all her might. Tears of pain filled her eyes, but she didn't dare move.

Everything was silent. Po was listening and watching for any sign of her. For a split second, Anna thought he knew she was there and was only playing with her, letting her believe in her victory before actually catching her. Then a sudden revelation occurred inside of her: she had already won. She had gotten what she needed, and Po wouldn't catch her. Not today. She had been very lucky, and the castle itself seemed to help her out.

This conviction gave her the strength to remain still, leaning on her terribly aching knee until the window finally closed.

Relieved, Anna waited a couple of heartbeats and started

moving down. She had to hurry. She was still an intruder and a rule-breaker. She deserved death just for getting on the castle grounds, not to mention the things she'd stolen. Being lucky was good, but it was also necessary to act upon it; otherwise, the moment would be lost, and luck would end as unexpectedly and quickly as it had started.

Trying to be as fast and silent as possible, she kept sliding down the drain, painfully bruising her knees and elbows. A couple of spells would have eased her pain at once, but she was so concentrated on her escape that it didn't even occur to her to use them until she finally reached the ground. Once there, she healed the worst of her wounds and carefully peered out of the drain.

The garden was empty and quiet. The sun had already set, and the safety of darkness slowly enveloped the earth.

Several feet away, on her right, Anna spotted the dark round entrance to the neighboring donjon. Tense and alert, she slid alongside the wall toward it.

The doorway looked empty. Anna stepped into it and exhaled, wiping her slimy aching hands on her skirt.

Out of nowhere, a rough hand covered her mouth. Before she could react, she was caught from behind, both her arms trapped. Her scream died away in the firm grip of the hand. She was lifted upward and dragged away into the darkness.

Kateryna Kei

Her captor moved with a rapid, silent pace. Uselessly struggling to free herself, Anna heard a door close behind them, and then her feet touched the ground. She was turned to face her captor and finally released. With both hands, she pushed him hard in the chest and hissed threateningly, "Do not ever do that again!"

A low chuckle came from the darkness. "You think you can resist?"

His voice was quiet, but his strong northern accent made Anna's heart skip a bit.

Her eyes were slowly adjusting to the darkness, and she distinguished his tall, broad-shouldered silhouette before her. She angrily crossed her arms over her chest, "Underestimating your opponent?"

A velvety laughter came from his chest, sending a shiver down Anna's spine. "I will take the risk ..."

Anna almost puffed with indignation, but before she could react, his strong arms closed around her and his lips pressed against hers.

Anna tried to push him away, but he was too strong, and her effort was wasted. His lips were soft and warm, and her body responded on its own accord. Her anger drowned in a burning wave of new feelings that swept her off her feet. His beard tickled her face, and his skin smelled like the sea. Anna felt the world turning upside down around her and instinctively grasped his shirt, completely abandoning herself to his lips.

A sudden knock on the door right behind her seemed thunder-loud. Anna nearly jumped, abruptly pulled back to reality.

The man let her go. He noiselessly removed his shirt and tossed it away.

"NAY!" Anna mouthed soundlessly, instantly guessing who was behind the door.

There seemed to be no way for him to hear her silent exclamation. Fast and gracious, he reached for the door.

Panic-stricken, Anna reacted instinctively. She slid back to the wall and froze, expecting the worst. Her eyes wide, she pressed herself hard against the cold stone, watching the door open inward toward her. It was only a dozen inches from her left shoulder! She stopped breathing, petrified.

"King Raven," she heard Po's falsely resigned voice say, and she shifted her glance from the door to her captor. Her heart leapt. Lit by Po's torch, the green-eyed captain stood in front of her. Straight, slim, and muscled, he looked stunningly handsome. His long, sunburnt hair fell freely across his tanned shoulders. The sight of his bare muscled chest, and the smell of him made Anna's knees go weak. The memory of his kiss was still fresh on her lips, and a storm of unknown feelings raged inside her as she stood there, pressed against the rough wall, unable to move or to take her eyes off of him.

"Evening, Po," Raven answered, annoyed, without looking at Anna. "I hope you have a valuable reason for disturbing me when I'm getting ready to sleep, especially given that the queen didn't bother to send a woman to warm my bed ..."

"Indeed, sir, my reason is valuable enough. A candlemark ago, something precious was stolen from the castle."

Raven coldly raised his brow. "What is my role in it? The few people who came with me to the castle are fast asleep under the effect of your excellent wine. As for me, you personally escorted me here, and since then I haven't left the donjon."

"Oh nay!" Po exclaimed, positively revolted. "I have never suspected you! Excuse me for this misunderstanding! But my duty is to find the robber, and I must ask you whether you have heard or seen somebody or something."

Raven thought for a while, and Anna's heart stopped beating, but then he shook his head, and his hair moved. Anna shivered. She couldn't avert her gaze from him.

"I didn't see anyone. As for sounds, honestly, I wasn't really listening … sorry. But what was stolen?"

"A very valuable possession of the queen's," the main priest answered importantly.

"Oh, I see," Raven nodded. Thoughtful, he ran his hand over his beard.

"I would love to help you, but I really don't see how. Maybe you can tell me whether this secret thing is easily noticeable?"

"Nay, it is small enough to hide inside a pocket," Po answered.

Raven shrugged impatiently. "Well, I already told you that I have seen nothing. But if you insist, you may search my room and my clothes."

Anna's jaw dropped in a silent gasp. She helplessly rolled her eyes at him, wishing he would hear her thoughts. But he just stood there in front of her, calm and serious, his attention entirely focused on Po, as if she didn't even exist. Usually, she would have found it annoying, but at that moment, she was too scared to think.

To her greatest relief, Po answered, "Nay, thank you. I trust your word. Good night, King Raven. I'll do my best to provide you with a woman."

Raven's face remained impassive. He slightly bowed his head, his eyes fixed on the priest. "I appreciate that. Good night, Po."

Anna heard Po's footsteps going away. Only when Raven locked the door did she allow herself to exhale.

Moving easily in the dark, Raven lit a torch and several candles. Then he turned to look at Anna, amusement dancing in his eyes.

"Seems like you're in trouble." His eyes raked her over as he added, "Does your queen hide her possessions in the mud?"

Anna automatically followed his glance and blushed furiously. She was a complete mess, covered in a mixture of dust and slime from head to toe, and her gown was torn in several places during her climb. It was deeply frustrating. She wished their first meeting had happened under different, more advantageous circumstances. She lifted her chin and retorted, "Well, the mud didn't stop you from kissing me, did it?"

She instantly regretted having said that. The memory of the kiss dangerously swayed her self-control, but he only laughed.

"You really think the imprints of your hands on my shirt would stop me?"

She threw a quick glance at her hands. They were very dirty and badly scratched. He had been aware of it all along—he removed his shirt before opening the door to hide her presence from Po. "Why did you cover up for me?"

His brow arched in surprise. "Would you rather I gave you away?"

She shook her head, feeling slightly disappointed; she was hoping to hear something else.

He walked to the bed and sat on it.

"What did you steal anyway?"

Anna felt even more awkward. She shrugged, recalling her

recent discoveries. "Things that belonged to my parents ..."

His green eyes watched her expectantly. His curiosity was not satisfied.

Anna bit her lip, wondering whether it was wise to follow the urge to talk to him about her parents. She had never talked about them to anyone but Nim. This topic was very intimate and dangerous. At the same time, her heart was telling her that she could trust him, and she felt a surge of panic realizing that, above all, she *wanted* to trust him.

He waited patiently, watching her.

Anna sighed. After all, he had the right to know—he had just saved her from Po! Resolved, she walked to the bed and, stopping at what seemed to be a reasonable distance from the man, emptied her pockets onto it.

"My mother's intercepted letters, a family portrait, my mother's hair, a dagger, and a ring," she explained, trying to sound casual and carefully avoiding his glance. "My father's ring," she added, turning it in her fingers. Faint lines on its surface represented the coat of arms of Ronen's family.

He watched very attentively, and then offered, "You can sit down."

Anna blinked, distracted. He was smiling at her.

Trying to sound casual, she reminded him, "My gown is dirty."

His smile revealed perfect white teeth. "Who cares?"

Anna rolled her eyes at him, but he wasn't teasing. Somewhat confused, she grinned back and carefully sat on the edge of the bed.

Raven didn't move, all the while looking down at the stolen objects.

"May I have a look?" he asked, and Anna nodded.

She watched him in silence as he examined the curl, the portrait, and the ring.

He carefully unwrapped the dagger and looked at it. "Did it belong to your father?"

"I don't think so. It probably killed my father, and it is still covered with blood …" she stated, shivering with revulsion.

Raven gently removed the scabbard and looked at the blade. Then he suddenly smelled it and looked back at Anna. "It's a woman's blood. The blade killed her by piercing her heart."

Anna stared. "How do you know?"

It was a prohibited question. He instantly averted his gaze and deliberated for some time whether it was safe to tell her the truth at this early stage.

When she thought he would never answer, he suddenly looked her straight in the eyes and whispered, "I am a raven."

Anna's eyes widened with awe. Understanding dawned on her face, and she beamed, happy to share his secret.

Looking into her blazing blue eyes, he knew she would never betray him. Her reaction made the whole experience of sharing secrets with her exciting.

"Po killed your parents." It was a guess, but not a question.

Anna's smile vanished, and her dust-covered face turned serious again. "I think so. We came here to find the truth. Po was in love with my mother, but she rejected him and married my father … Hey, do you feel it too?" She had a weird sensation that she was somehow transmitting him her feelings and pictures from her mind. Moreover, she was sensing his reaction much more intently than ever before, as if she had known him forever.

He gave her a crooked smile. "Aye, I do … Weird, isn't it?"

"How are you doing it? I've never experienced anything like it before!"

He arched his brow. "I'm not doing anything! I swear!"

Anna chortled at his sincere, innocent stare.

"I guess it's because it's you and me ..." he mused.

Her eyes scorched from under her lashes. "The bond ..." she hinted.

"Aye ..." he nodded, his tone thick with implications.

Her blue eyes sparkled with childish excitement. "Do you still feel it just as strong as the first time?"

Raven's eyes narrowed. "Why are you asking if you already know the answer?"

Anna blushed but did not skulk. "Just wanted to hear it from you ..."

His smile became smug as he took his time answering. His green eyes locked with hers. "Aye. I do feel this connection between the two of us as much as you do, and it is as strong as it was when our eyes first met."

Still rose-faced, Anna beamed.

"The mud on your face looks cute when you blush like that," he teased.

She frowned in resentment, but before she had time to retort, he changed the subject. "So, you were saying that your mother rebuffed Po ... Go on. I'm curious."

Anna looked at his boyish smirk. She could not be mad at him. With a heavy sigh, she gave up, and it only amused him more.

She rubbed her forehead, trying to bring some order to her thoughts, and then resumed her tale. "Po killed my mother's family and took control of the kingdom. According to the letters, he was so jealous that he decided to go as far as destroying my father's soul so that Mother would lose him forever."

Raven's brow puckered, and he shook his head. "Sorry, you lost me here ... Are you telling me that a soul can be destroyed?"

Anna nodded seriously. "It's dark and advanced magic. It

makes someone disappear completely from the world. They cease to exist. They cannot return, and there is no afterlife for them. It's bad for anyone, but for my parents, it would have been even worse. They shared a soul ..." she blushed and threw him a loaded look, "like us ..."

Raven didn't laugh. His emerald eyes widened with horror. "That's what Po did to them?"

Anna shrugged. "I think he tried but failed. Both my parents died, and according to Nim, my mother did it willingly."

"So you are a princess," he mused after a while. "A foreign princess who is my true love ..." His eyes became dreamy. "I remembered it the moment I saw you."

He could not have said it better. Anna nodded. "So did I ..."

"You know, when I was a child, our rune caster foretold a prophecy for me and my twin brother. He said I would find my true love in a foreign country ..."

Looking into his eyes, Anna felt every emotion he was trying to communicate to her, and it was marvelous. She vividly imagined the long, lined face of the rune caster, lit by the firelight. Suddenly, the rest of the prophecy echoed in her mind and sent a cold shiver down her spine, *"You will lose each other forever. Centuries of unbearable pain and suffering await you."*

Anna felt like crying. Now that Raven was with her, the horrors from the prophecy appeared under a different angle, so much more real and scary.

"Did he tell you we were ... doomed?" she whispered.

He didn't avert his gaze but nodded. So they were on the same page.

Aware of their bond with every cell of their bodies, they both knew there was no way back. And even if there was, neither of them would have ever chosen it. Neither would ever be able to live without the other. They were one, and breaking apart would be just as painful as tearing apart a living person. It seemed unbelievable that they could have lived all that time without knowing each other.

Raven broke the silence first. "I will fight!" he vowed, his eyes sparkling with determination. "You?"

His sudden hope illuminated all of Anna's being. His determination washed over her, and she echoed, "I will!"

A boyish smile lit Raven's face, and Anna felt just as happy. He offered her his hand, and she beamed as her fingers touched his rough palm. They just watched each other, enjoying the long-forgotten feelings.

"Damn it!" muttered Raven, suddenly bending toward her and catching her by the waist.

Anna gasped. Before she knew it, she was sitting on his lap. She flung her arm around his neck and smiled. "You seem to like my mud?"

He hugged her to his chest. "Definitely …" He slowly covered her mouth with his.

Neither of them had ever experienced anything like it before. Their blazing sensations intertwined, exploding in a torrent of fire and joy. They were two in one and one in two, they were burning for each other, transforming, appeasing and exciting one another. It was so marvelous that they wished it would never end.

Raven was the first to recover. Ending the kiss, he whispered, "Anna, I swear I'll fight for you as long as my soul exists."

She looked at him, panting. "Promise me that you won't let your soul die."

He held her gaze and slowly nodded. "I promise."

Anna knew he would do anything to keep his promise, and it made her feel less scared of their common future. She slid her hands into the golden silk of his hair. It was smooth and slightly cool, and it felt so nice in her hands that she grinned happily. "How could we have lived apart all these years?"

He shrugged, holding her tighter against his chest. "I guess we forgot somehow ..."

He watched her face and wished it would never end. "Stay with me," he whispered finally.

Her hands stopped moving, and her blue gaze became serious. She suddenly remembered where she was and why. Misery washed over her as she considered it for a while, torn between the temptation to stay and the right thing to do.

The sense won, and she shook her head, unable to hide her disappointment.

"The castle is not safe. Po can come back at any moment to spy on you, and if he catches us together ..." This thought sent a cold shiver down her spine.

Raven looked unconvinced.

Wincing, Anna took his face with both her hands and looked into the emerald depths of his eyes. She needed him to understand the danger of the situation.

"We are on his territory, and he is a very powerful magician. I've done enough tonight to get myself killed on the spot."

Raven weighed every sentence obediently.

"All right," he muttered, not even trying to hide his disappointment, and released Anna from his grip. "I'll help you then ..."

He looked like a boy whose favorite toy had been taken away, and Anna shared his feelings entirely. She did not want to leave him. It felt too good sitting in his lap, hugging him, and touching his hair. She wanted to kiss him again, to press herself against him, forgetting everything. Instead, she stood up and stepped away from him, trying at least not to make it even harder.

He closed his eyes, as if listening to his thoughts. Anna stood silent, waiting patiently. Finally, he looked up at her. "Do you know how to climb?"

"Aye," she answered, recalling the drain.

"Good."

He bent down and pulled out a roll of rope from under the bed. "Let's go. The way is free."

Anna quickly gathered all the things she had stolen, and they stepped into the night.

He found the stairs and led the way up in complete darkness, firmly holding her by the hand. His movements were light, quick, and noiseless, and Anna imagined how dangerous he would be in battle. She couldn't stop admiring him.

Finally, she saw his silhouette against the starlit sky. The gentle breeze moved her hair, caressing her skin. They were on the very top of the donjon. The castle itself shone like a star, and on the perfectly polished marble surface, Anna could see their reflection.

Raven turned to look at her. "Anna, will I see you tomorrow? I'll stay on the ship for the night."

She beamed with excitement. "You will take me to your ship?"

He smiled and nodded. "Just tell me where I can pick you up."

Sweet anticipation filled her as she tried to think of a safe place. Meanwhile, Raven tied the rope around a stone buttress and checked it.

"North from the port, the coast is rocky. There is a natural archway on top called the Star Gate. It can be seen from afar. Under the archway, there is a small bay."

Raven's eyes widened. "The Star Gate ..." he repeated like an echo. "I'll be there at nightfall."

"What if there is a feast or something?"

He shrugged and repeated, "I'll be there."

The shade of the bird fell upon the wall. Anna looked up and saw the raven making silent circles above them.

"Thank you," she whispered, projecting her thoughts toward him. The raven didn't react, but she was sure he heard her.

"He says you're welcome!" whispered the man, grinning. "Oh, and I have to give this back to you …"

Guiltily averting his gaze, he pulled out of his pocket the bracelet with her magical sign.

"He brought it to me," he explained, gesturing toward the soaring bird. "That's how I knew your name … sorry …"

Moved and amused by his embarrassment, Anna had trouble suppressing a chuckle. She reached out and took his hand. Seizing the bracelet with her other hand, she put it around his wrist and carefully tied the leather straps. Then, turning his hand palm up, she bent down and kissed it.

When she looked up, his expression made her heart accelerate madly.

"You keep it," she whispered.

"I can't wait for tomorrow," he confessed. "You'd better go before I change my mind …"

She did. Taking the rope from his hands, she stepped on the edge of the wall and placed her legs onto it securely.

"Pull on it three times when you reach the ground," he whispered and quickly kissed her lips.

Anna started climbing.

It was harder than she expected. The wall seemed endless, and the polished marble was slippery. Anna painfully bumped her bruised knee against the wall before stopping her feet from sliding with a spell. She felt more and more tired, and her arms were terribly sore. When she thought she would groan with pain, her foot finally touched the ground. Stepping on the firm land, she felt her knees shaking. She pulled on the rope three times. It instantly rushed up.

She mentally called her horse, and relief washed over her when she heard the friendly clatter of hooves.

The black raven was still making large circles far above her.

"May the gods protect you!" she mentally called to him, thinking of her captain. Then she climbed in the saddle and rode home. And again, the farther she was from him, the harder it was to keep going.

By the time she got to their wooden forest hut, she was seriously considering turning back, and even Po's evil powers and all the risks seemed meaningless next to her strong need to be by Raven's side.

As she had expected, Nim was waiting for her. The fairy woman sat motionless outside among the branches.

Anna halted her horse and slid down from her saddle. She felt very happy and completely exhausted.

Nim watched her thoughtfully. It was not in her habit to yell or to show she was worried.

Fighting back her exhaustion, Anna blurted out excitedly, "Nim, it's unbelievable. I met him! We do share one soul! You know, we both felt it the moment our eyes met! Nim, it's so wonderful! It feels like … remembering something dear and deeply forgotten …"

Nim lifted up her hand, stopping Anna's torrent of words. Her lined face still looked impassive, but a smile played in her bright-blue eyes. She slid gracefully down from the tree and said, "Get in, child. I will take care of your horse. A cup of tea is waiting for you on the table. And don't even think of falling asleep before you tell me everything!"

Anna did as she was told. Shortly afterward, they were both sitting inside in front of a small fire, which made the simple room look cozy and intimate.

The tea had a refreshing effect on Anna and awoke her appetite. While she ate, she told Nim in detail everything that happened to her, as well as displaying her findings.

Nim threw back her beautiful golden hair, deep in thought. "We will know exactly what happened that night. I can make this old blood speak, but we have to wait until the moon is full."

Anna glanced at the small window. "Two more days. We have waited much longer ..."

Nim nodded and stood up.

"Try and get some sleep now. I'm going to the forest—we might need some special ingredients for that type of magic."

Anna looked up at her. "Am I forgiven?" she asked simply.

Nim gave her an affectionate smile. "Of course you are! Knowing your temper, I doubted you would obey for long. What matters is that you are back and alive. However, given your recent deeds, make sure you inform me about where you are going and why, in case you need help. Can you promise me that?"

Anna understood the seriousness of her request and nodded. "I promise."

Nim hugged her and kissed her good night, as usual. Even though Anna was no longer a child, they unanimously kept this tradition.

When Nim left, Anna curled up on her bed. She filled her lungs with the deliciously fresh night air and smiled, drifting away to the mysterious world of dreams.

Before leaving, Nim placed several spells around the hut. She needed to know if anyone tried to get close. Her protections had never failed yet, and she honestly doubted even the main priest would be able to break them, for her magic was a very ancient one, and no one else in the whole world knew it.

Satisfied, the fairy woman noiselessly hurried away. She had a lot to do, and wasting time was not a habit of hers.

The Nightmare

She was on a ship. The clean, wooden deck moved rhythmically under her feet, the salty air caressed her and toyed with her gown. Holding her hand in his, Raven showed her around, explaining the basics of sailing. She felt happy and whole, more in harmony with the world than ever before. She beamed. Suddenly, she noticed that a golden glow was emanating from both of them, illuminating everything in their immediate visibility. She stopped to make sure he saw it as well. Raven smiled and hugged her.

"We are a sun under the sun!"

She stepped on tiptoe and kissed him, savoring the sweet warmth of his lips. He pressed her safely to his chest, and she wished it would last forever.

"Let's sail away!" she wanted to ask him, when a deafening thunderbolt tore the sky apart. Anna panicked when she saw that the stern of the ship had caught fire.

"Wait for me here!" ordered Raven, letting go of her.

The next moment, she saw him running toward the fire.

The storm was raging around the ship. Heavy gray-and-violet clouds hung so low that the huge waves almost touched them.

Seized by a deep fear, Anna knew she had to get to Raven and ran after him.

The ship shook violently, and the cold, angry waves crashed on the deck. Anna was swept off her feet and washed back and out of the ship. She could not see Raven anymore. Holding to the ship with all her might, she called him again and again.

Her voice was too weak to overcome the uproar of the elements raging around her. Somehow, she knew that no one would come. She was lonely and helpless, fighting the ice-cold angry waves all by herself. The unmistakable sense of danger scorched her insides, but her body felt uncontrollable and light, as if it no longer belonged to her.

Yet there was no question of surrendering. After what seemed like an eternity, she got back to the ship and managed to stand up. Where was everyone? There was no crew, and there were no oars to control the ship. The sail was ripped by the wind and disappeared somewhere in the heavy blackness of the monstrous clouds.

She ran forward, and the darkness became more pungent as it thickened around her. She noticed that she was not glowing anymore, and it terrified her. She realized she was running in place, helpless. Soon, the darkness enveloped her completely. She couldn't see, but she kept calling Raven, struggling against her own helplessness.

Suddenly, another flash of lightning tore everything apart. The ship and the storm were no more. A ringing, hollow silence enveloped everything. Anna blinked and looked around. Only one object stood out from the surrounding dark void, suspended in the air. A scream of horror froze on Anna's lips—the silvery hilt of the dagger was emitting a sickening glow, and the ruby-eyed skull was gloating at her as fresh crimson blood glistened on the blade, a single drop forming on its tip. Paralyzed by fear, Anna watched the drop fall. It slowly turned in the air and caught the light, sparkling like a horrible ruby.

"RAVEN!"

Her own scream woke her. She was sobbing and drenched in cold sweat. Her body shook uncontrollably. It took her some time to realize that she was safe inside their tiny forest hut, in her own bed. The room was dark—apparently, it was still night outside. The fire was extinguished; only the coals glowed weakly, diffusing cozy warmth through the space.

"A nightmare, just a nightmare!" Anna repeated to herself, desperately trying to calm down.

It didn't work. The panic was still holding her with its ice-cold claws as she stood up. The horrifying dagger was lying on the table, along with the rest of her stolen objects, and the mere sight of it brought a new wave of panic over her. Fighting down a scream, Anna ran out of the hut into the blackened forest.

She mentally called Nim, as she badly needed her help.

Nim answered her call instantly, and in short order, Anna was crouching by her side, safely hidden in her arms.

Nim listened attentively to her somewhat incoherent story, gently stroking her hair. She knew what it meant—she had known it for years—yet she loved Anna too much to be able to make an objective decision. Would it be better to tell her the truth, or to keep her safely unaware of it? After all, Anna knew the prophecy about the terrible fate of their love, but the girl had been so happy telling Nim about it that bringing forward the hopelessness of the situation seemed incredibly cruel. After a moment of internal struggle, Nim decided not to ruin Anna's happiness, no matter how short lived it had to be.

She kissed the top of Anna's head and whispered, "There, there, try to calm down. Panic is a very bad ally."

Anna sobbed again like a child.

"You are safe now, and I'm sure your love is safe as well … try to think clearly."

Anna looked up at her and obediently wiped the wetness from her cheeks.

"Child, do not let the fear seize you. If you decided to fight, believe in yourself and use every single opportunity. Make the most of every moment!"

Anna nodded, determination growing in the depths of her blue eyes.

Nim loved the girl more than anyone else in this life, and the knowledge that Anna was fated to undergo a terrible suffering made her heart scream in pain.

"I promise I'll do all I can to help you," she said quietly. "Be strong and listen to your heart. Intuition is always the best ally!"

They talked for a while, trying to think of different possibilities and outcomes. Anna wasn't scared anymore. Instead, she felt strong, fiery determination burning inside her.

"I'll go home. We will meet tonight at the Star Gate, and I don't want to feel weak or sleepy," she announced finally, standing up.

Nim gave her a loving smile. "Of course. Use some lavender to stop the nightmares."

"Thank you, Nim. I love you."

Nim pretended that she was examining a plant to hide the tears that filled her old eyes. "I love you too, child."

Anna walked home slowly. Talking to Nim reassured and comforted her, yet the feeling of worry remained anchored in the pit of her stomach. If only she could see Raven, for just one moment, just to make sure he was okay! Without really knowing why, she found her horse and rode to the Star Gate.

The sea was smooth and quiet. The new day was slowly dawning, and the stars were fading above her. The archway called the Star Gate stood undisturbed on the jagged, rocky coast.

Anna dismounted and walked over to the structure. The windswept rock was cold under her hand, and Anna stood in silent admiration, sensing the particular, mysterious atmosphere of this place.

Peering out at the sea, she saw Raven's ship anchored in front of the beach. Farther to the left was the white castle, where she had left Raven in the evening. Everything was quiet and sleepy in the grayish light of the dawning day. A day-long wait lay in front of her before she would finally be with Raven again.

Anna sighed and turned to leave when a croak tore the silence apart, making her jump. His head slightly tilted to the right, the big black raven looked down at her from the top of the Star Gate.

Anna couldn't help grinning. She was so happy to see the bird!

"When did you get here?" she asked.

The bird croaked mockingly.

"Where is Raven?" Anna asked in a whisper, unable to hide her worry. "Is he safe?"

The raven remained motionless for several long seconds, thoughtfully looking at her with his beetle-like eyes.

Anna stared back, trying to guess the answer.

Then he took off and flew toward her, hovering in midair and waiting for her to hold out her arm. As she did so, the bird landed on her wrist and met her eyes.

But instead of talking to her like most animals did, the bird's dark glance seemed to force its way into the depth of Anna's mind, and Anna gasped, suddenly seeing the answer in real time.

She was in the castle, in the room where Raven had brought her several candlemarks ago. She recognized the wooden door, the simple furniture, and the large bed. Raven was lying there, fast asleep. His fair hair fell on the pillow, and his muscled back looked even more tanned against the whiteness of the blankets.

As if he felt Anna's glance, he suddenly rolled onto his back and opened his eyes, looking back at her. His lips parted in a sleepy smirk. Then he winked at her, and Anna blushed, feeling like she'd been caught spying. She blinked, and the connection broke.

The bird croaked mockingly and flew away.

Her heart pounded in her chest as Anna watched him soar above the waves. She was beaming. Her worries were gone, and she even regretted her embarrassment, burning to see Raven again. She waved goodbye to the bird, thanking him with all her heart, and headed back home.

THE TWINS

Raven spent most of the day in the castle with three of his men. They were invited to attend Queen Elena's various entertainments and midday meal. The servants were attentive to them, but the queen did not even look their way. At the same time, the Vikings knew that they were being watched closely all the time. It was done masterfully—they were followed by different people who looked like they were doing other things, but they were experienced warriors and not easily fooled. They decided to play along as happy guests and to just observe.

The atmosphere in the castle was odd. Everything was excessive: flatteries and compliments, people's clothing and jewelry, meals and luxurious interiors. Raven thought that it looked like a huge living puppet play, wherein not a single smile was genuine. The queen spent her whole day entertaining herself, as if nothing existed beyond the castle walls.

In the evening, Raven was finally able to go back to his ship, but for a very limited time—Queen Elena was expecting him for dinner.

When the supplies they had bought at the market were properly stored, Raven walked to the bow where his brother, Olaf, sat.

Olaf and Raven were twins. It was an important strategic asset; for this reason, they never appeared together in foreign countries and cities that they visited.

Olaf pulled out his water flask and moved over on the bench to make some room for Raven.

"So how was it, brother?"

"I met her."

Olaf's hand with the flask froze on its way to his mouth, and his face went pale. He understood. For a couple of heartbeats, he searched Raven's face, as if he was hoping that his brother was joking. Then he asked, "Is she really worth it?"

Raven smiled. Years ago, he and Olaf had heard the prophecy about their respective futures. Raven was promised centuries of unbearable pain and suffering after having lost his true love, and Olaf was persuaded that, in this case, it was better not to meet her at all. Raven loved his brother very much but could not agree with him, especially after having met Anna. It was hard to describe how he felt, for the words "whole" and "happy" could not express it in the full measure. He had become a completely new being; Anna's love was burning inside of him, giving him joy and strength. He was bound to Anna by invisible and unbreakable bonds, and this connection ran soul-deep. They were united by something bigger than life, by something beautiful that was at the core of the universe. They were destined to meet each other, no matter what. It was unavoidable, and in his heart, Raven hoped that, against the odds, this beautiful connection between them would survive even the prophecy, and they would be together forever.

"Trust me, she is."

Olaf looked like he wanted to add something, but he only heaved a sigh.

"I am meeting her tonight at the Star Gate. Will you help me, please?"

Olaf nodded. "You know I will. What do you want me to do?"

"Spend this night in the castle instead of me. I want to wed her under the Star Gate—it would be good to have the ancient magic helping us as well."

"So you decided to fight against the prophecy?"

"Aye. Anna will fight with me."

"Anna ..."

Raven caught his brother's hand.

"Olaf, please, try to understand: the prophecy is not Anna's fault. We are in it together, she and I, and *we* decided to fight. We will win or fail, but whatever the outcome, we will do it together."

Olaf chuckled bitterly. "How do you expect everyone to accept her?"

Raven fell silent. He hadn't thought about that. Olaf was right—as a king, he was free to choose his wife, but it did not mean that his people would respect her and treat her as their queen.

"I will tell them the truth. I will tell them that it is all part of the prophecy about me, that she is my true love and she shares my soul. Then she will win everyone's respect."

Olaf knew he was losing the battle. More out of exasperation than anything else, he voiced his last argument. "But what of our people? You would put them in danger for her?"

Raven flinched. It was a prohibited blow. He feared more than anything that someone would have to die or suffer because of him. He was even feeling uncomfortable sending Olaf to the castle for the night. But what other choice did he have? He could not live without Anna.

"I will do anything in my power to keep you and all my men safe. If we have to leave in a hurry, so be it—I will come back for Anna on my own."

Olaf shook his head. "That's not what I mean. What will come of our people if something happens to you?"

Raven could feel his brother's deep worry. He had spent years trying to find something that would comfort his brother and his mother, his closest family, the two people apart from the rune caster who had heard the prophecy entirely, but no argument would work. He hated causing them pain.

"Our people are lucky—if something happens to me, they have you. As for me, I will do my best to protect all of you and Anna. That's what I was named king for. Also, I think you are right. I feel danger here, and I'd better warn everyone about it."

His heart heavy, Olaf said nothing, his water flask long since forgotten.

Without further waiting, Raven gathered all his men to discuss the situation. They were a team, and they trusted each other with their lives, so it was only natural to let everyone speak their mind and participate in the decision-making process.

"I do not think we will get any agreement from them. Their queen's word is useless, and I don't like their priests," Ari said. Ari had been Raven's father's best friend. He was very much a warrior, not a negotiator, and he hated everything complicated and elaborate.

"That's my opinion as well," Orm nodded. Orm was also a very good storyteller, and Raven valued his insight.

"The queen is controlled by the priests, but I'm curious to see how the negotiations will go," Sveinn stated with his usual calm.

"I agree with all of you. I don't trust the queen, or her men either," Raven told them. "In addition, I feel that we are in danger here, even though I can see neither the reason nor the proof of it."

"We won't leave like cowards, without having done what we came for!" Kirk objected.

"We have to try and get that wood," Ottar added. "If Coenred attacks, we will be in trouble without it."

Raven lifted up his hand to stop them. "Wait! I am not suggesting that we should leave before we have tried to negotiate. I only want to warn all of you."

Kirk waved his hand dismissively. "We have seen battles and danger. I bet they have nothing new here!"

"They have magic," Raven replied.

"Magic?"

"So what?" Kirk wasn't impressed. "Magicians are humans, too. They can be killed with an axe."

Raven wasn't so sure about that. Kirk was underestimating an enemy that they knew almost nothing about, and that was dangerous. Fortunately, most of the Vikings were slightly more reasonable.

"You shouldn't underestimate them, Kirk," Helgi intervened. "I heard magicians are sometimes capable of terrible things. Aren't they, Orm?"

Orm agreed and instantly named several examples.

It did not scare the Vikings much, and Raven felt the same way. They had never seen magic, apart from the rune casting, so it was very hard to take it seriously. However, he had no time to do anything about it at the moment, and it was probably better this way—fear could be incapacitating, and that was definitely something none of them needed.

"There is something else I need to tell you. You all remember the rune caster's prophecy that made me your king?"

Everyone remembered. It was quite an ordeal at the time, as Raven—an underage boy and the second of the twins—had been suggested as a successor to his dead father, to win the war against the same evil Foreigners that were threatening them now. The prophecy did not lie—to everyone's surprise, Raven had won the war back then. However, none of them knew the second part of it—about Raven's true love and everything that was supposed to happen afterward.

Raven decided that they did not need to know the scary part of it. What use could it be to them anyway? But he told them that he was fated to find his true love and that he had just met her and was intending to wed her.

His men's reaction was a pleasant surprise—they congratulated and encouraged him.

"I hope she is beautiful—"

"She'd better be!"

"I'm sure she is!"

"Then take her, before someone else decides to steal her from you!"

"Go and enjoy her company, Konungr[*]! You deserve it! Olaf will go to the castle instead of you, won't you, Olaf?"

Olaf nodded, avoiding everyone's glance. "You can count on me."

Apart from Raven, no one noticed Olaf's unease.

While Olaf was getting dressed in Raven's clothes, five men took their place in the small boat. They were going to the castle with Olaf.

Olaf's heart was heavy as he stepped into the boat. He took his brother's hand. "Hrafn[**] ..." He wanted to say so many things but was suddenly at a loss for words.

Raven patted his shoulder. "I'll come and take your place in the morning, brother."

"Be careful, please."

---

[*] Konungr—king (Old Norse)
[**] Hrafn—Norse version of Raven

THE STAR GATE

Anna was back at the Star Gate before sunset, having slept most of the day away. When Nim woke her, she forced herself to eat and hurried out afterward. Nim watched with mixed feelings as she rode away. She was wise enough to accept anything, especially if it made Anna happy. On the other hand, Anna was her everything, the daughter she'd never had, and she couldn't help feeling deeply annoyed by the appearance of this man. With his abrupt arrival into their lives, the prophecy was coming to fruition, and danger was ominously close.

Meanwhile, Anna hurried her horse to the Star Gate, unable to wait any longer. Patience was not a virtue of hers; she could hardly imagine a worse punishment than being forced to wait.

When she arrived, she let her horse go and sat on the grass, leaning back against the archway. She could see the castle and the ship from where she sat, but nothing was happening at either location.

Soon, she started to worry again. What if Raven could not manage to get out of the castle? Or what if something else, even more terrible, had happened? Struggling to calm herself, she kept waiting, jumping at every sound.

The sun took an eternity to disappear, and for the first time, Anna was urging it on instead of simply admiring it.

Finally, the darkness fell, and Anna's heart gave a happy

leap as she spotted a tiny boat on the surface of the sea, right behind the ship. She watched it coming forward, and when she was positive it was moving toward her, she ran down the rocky path to the water. The urge to see Raven was burning her from the inside out.

Raven rowed into the bay. He smiled when he saw Anna, impatience etched on her face.

"Don't get into the water," he called. "I'll come to you."

She couldn't wait any longer. The moment he stepped into the water to pull the boat onto the sand, Anna threw herself into his arms.

Raven laughed and hugged her, the boat forgotten.

"Raven," she breathed, savoring the feeling of him. "You are safe!"

"Of course I am, but I enjoyed you checking in on me."

Anna's face went red with embarrassment. "Sorry, I had a nightmare …"

Raven laughed and cupped her face with his hand. "It's all right. You share my soul, and I have no secrets from you."

Suddenly, Anna felt shy. "Neither do I. Now that you brought it up, though, I do want to know everything about you."

Raven's lips parted in a crooked smile. "I will satisfy your curiosity, but first, I need to kiss you."

His lips brushed against hers very lightly, teasing her. She slid her arms around his neck and pressed herself to him, deepening the kiss. She wanted him closer, for only then did she feel whole and right. Kissing him was invigorating—the touch of his lips set her feelings on fire and made her heart plummet to her toes.

Some time later, when they were finally able to pull away from each other ever so slightly, Raven glanced up, trying to steady his breath. His glance fell on the archway. It was bathed in the silvery moonlight, motionless and proud.

"So that's the famous Star Gate," he mused, his eyes sparkling with fascination. "Can we get closer?"

"Sure."

They climbed the rocky path and stopped in front of the archway. The dark stones seemed alive, observing them in silence.

Raven ran his hand over its side, his expression revealing a quiet admiration.

"For my people, this Gate is legendary," he said, softly.

Anna raised her brow in surprise. "Why?"

He shrugged. "It is said that a great hero of old times, legendary through his deeds, wed his beloved by passing under it. They lived in happiness and glory and had a lot of children. The Star Gate is believed to be a token of lasting and happy love."

A shiver ran down Anna's spine. She stared at Raven, lost for words.

A glimmer of hope played in Raven's emerald eyes. He offered her his hand, palm up. "Anna, will you pass under it with me?" His voice came out hoarse, betraying his emotions.

Anna's heart somersaulted in her chest, and tears of happiness filled her eyes. She covered his hand with hers and nodded, "Aye."

A breathtaking smile overtook Raven's face, his eyes shining with so much love that Anna's knees felt weak.

Hand in hand, they slowly stepped under the archway. Stopping there, they looked at the stone arch above them, and then back at each other. Sheer joy and excitement was written on Raven's face, and Anna shared his emotions. Raven's hand slid around Anna's waist. He slowly bent his head and kissed her. She kissed him back with all the passion she felt for him, wishing with all her might the magic of the ancient archway would work for them as well. They would have to fight for their love against destiny itself, and they needed all the help they could get.

When Raven and Anna finally stepped out from under the archway, they were both beaming. The whole world seemed different somehow. In addition to their bond, they were now united through an old pagan wedding; the rocks, moon, stars, and sea were their witnesses.

"It's the most romantic wedding ever!" Anna whispered.

Raven laughed, his white teeth glistening in the dark.

"That's how I dreamt it to be."

Two Parts of a Soul

The main priest woke up with a jolt. His whole body felt tense, and his chest was heaving. Old, unpleasant memories, which he sometimes wished he could erase, had come back in his dream once again.

The sickeningly soft and kind voice of his first master still echoed in his mind.

"Randi, my handsome boy, you certainly want to please me, don't you? I wish you well, my dear boy, you know it!"

Po rubbed his face with his hands. He did not want to remember his childhood. That was another life, finished, and wiped away. The life of a young boy named Randi, a boy only Po remembered. Poverty, hunger, and deprivation had been his family's everyday life for generations. Randi despised them all for their attitude and values; he loathed them with his whole being. Even as a child, he wished he were not one of them. He knew that there were other possibilities—there were smarter, richer, cleaner people who could have everything, and Randi desperately wanted to be one of them. When he figured that out, he refused to work in the mine with his stupid father and filthy brothers, and no argument or thrashing could make him change his mind. So his father sold him to his first and only master, a fat, kind-faced, rich priest who loved young handsome boys.

Randi had been very happy about it at first; he was given a chance at a better life with enough food and clean clothes, but his delight was short-lived. The priest beat and abused him, preaching all the time that it was all for Randi's own good, for only through pain could he gain "the ultimate wisdom." Randi was eleven back then and had a very hard time believing it.

For other priests, too, Randi was but a slave. They found it hilarious to humiliate him.

Back then, Randi felt more miserable than ever. All his hopes for a better life were broken and trampled into the mud. He had food and clean clothes, but he felt filthier than ever and even poorer, for even his own body no longer belonged to him. There was no salvation and no going back; Randi had sworn that he would never go back to his repugnant family, and the remaining shards of his pride would not allow him to do it anyway. Life lost all attraction; it was one long disgusting torture.

Randi wished he could die, but his master knew exactly when to stop. His torture and abuse were never enough to keep the boy in bed for more than one day, let alone kill him. It was the period of Randi's biggest weakness; memories of it still made him feel bitter shame and self-hatred, along with overwhelming misery and exasperation. He had almost lost himself back then.

However, his much-needed salvation came unexpectedly. Determined to make his master kill him, Randi purposefully walked into his chambers when he was not allowed to and saw the fat priest doing magic. A ball of fire that his master produced in a flicker of his hand was floating in the air and moving whenever the priest wanted it to. Randi froze, staring at the scene, impressed to the very core of his being. He had never seen anything like it—mysterious, capricious, and powerful. Randi knew instantly that it was exactly what he needed, what he had been looking for. It was the perfect answer to all his problems and suffering.

Mesmerized by the sight, the boy forgot all caution. The priest's velvety voice brought him back to reality. Randi blinked, no longer so sure whether he still wanted to die. However, seeing the boy's stunned look, his master mistook it for fear and was only pleased. Randi got out with a flogging that put him in bed for three days, but it did not matter anymore—the fire of hope was slowly starting to burn inside him, warming his very soul and giving a sense of purpose to his miserable life. He needed magic no matter what; he had to have it at any cost.

Magic opened a new door for Randi. It became his light, his inspiration, and his desire. It gave him the strength to endure everything. He started avidly learning everything he could, from the art of pain and torture to ruse and manipulation; he silently accepted everything and did the most disgusting things to satisfy his stupid master. At night, when his master was sound asleep, Randi would sneak into a forbidden cabinet to read and learn.

He learned and practiced as much as he could, and he was patient enough to make sure no one discovered what he was doing until he was ready. It only made his revenge sweeter—the memory of his master's terrified face and girlish whimpering when Randi slowly tortured him still made him smile.

Fortunately, Randi and the ghosts of the past did not bother Po very often, but when they did, Po felt weak and helpless. He hated these feelings. To stifle them, he had to spend some time reminding himself how much he had achieved, how many lives were completely under his control, how easily he could torture and kill anyone, and most importantly, he had to remind himself that no one would ever hurt and humiliate him again.

Po walked to the large mirror. His body was young and perfect; it bore no scar or sign of pain. It showed no trace of age. He was able to wipe it all away with magic. He had personally tortured and killed everyone who ever dared to cause him pain, including his father and brothers. He did not bother going after his mother and sister; they were scum and not worth his attention. Over fifty years had passed since then, so they were most likely dead. He did not want to have anything to do with these illiterate, dust-covered people with sunken faces and extinguished eyes. The old mistreated slave boy was gone. Instead, a new man was born: smart, strong, and deadly, the man who was rightfully feared and respected, the most powerful magician.

Putting on his white robes, Po thought that there was one thing that his master had gotten right after all: pain and fear were, by far, the best tools for achieving anything. The world was divided between the strong and the weak. The strong played with the weak and used them as they wanted. They could give the weak some joy or make them writhe in pain. They could shape the lives and destinies of the weak. It was their natural right. The strongest always won, and this was only fair. Someone who was born weak could become strong, like Po had, if he had the guts for it. As for others—miserable, gutless creatures—they only deserved to serve, to be manipulated; their bodies, lives, and even souls rightfully belonging to those who were stronger and more intelligent.

Po turned away from the mirror and walked to the table. His favorite big ruby gleamed in the moonlight. The stone looked alive, as if it were watching the priest, as if it knew all his thoughts and deepest secrets and was mocking him for his weakness, for what he had done once.

It suddenly made Po feel angry. He took the ruby and held it in his hand in front of him.

"I won! I won over all of them!" he hissed at the ruby. "It was all for magic! Do you hear? Magic is worth all of it!"

Two Parts of a Soul

He slammed the ruby back on the table, not entirely convinced that the mysterious stone was satisfied by his explanation.

"I'll prove it to you now that Melaina is back," he promised the ruby and sat down.

Somehow, his thoughts of Melaina only strengthened the feeling of bitterness, but Po managed to shut it away so it wouldn't disturb him from planning for the future. The new game had just begun, and he was eager to play it.

He recalled the girl he'd seen back at the ceremony. There was something disturbing about her face, something he could not quite put a finger on. She looked like she was having an epiphany of some sort. Was it the raven's appearance that she had interpreted as an omen? Melaina had come back as this new girl, and she must have changed. Po suddenly realized that he knew very little about her.

His gaze traveled over the objects on his table and stopped on a small leather bag. He took it and opened it. Human finger bones rattled inside. Of course, Po had other tools for divination, but this particular set of bones, which he had personally taken from his enemies, including his father, brothers, and his master, seemed most appropriate to use after the nightmare. The bones were yet more proof of Po's strength, of his triumph over those who had dared to abuse and humiliate him.

Po slid his hand inside the bag and lovingly caressed the bones, formulating his question, then threw them on the table in front of him. He carefully read the answer they were showing, starting from the top.

Her name was Anna. She was Melaina's daughter. She had a guardian who had managed to hide her from Po until now, and she was a talented witch.

Po's lips parted in a satisfied grin. How fitting! She was still exactly the woman he needed. The main priest felt she was bright and pure. She would allow him to achieve even greater power, for the magic of her ancestors ran through her blood. Finally, she would fully belong to him!

Po was so impatient to learn more that he didn't even take the time to savor the vision of his victory. His white hand froze over the bones spread out on the table as his beautiful vision shattered, bringing forward the very same feeling of agony that he had experienced almost twenty years ago. Anna was in love. Someone else had just taken her from Po.

"Nay, nay, NAAAAY!" The main priest's angry growl echoed through the room and the adjacent corridor, waking some of the priests downstairs.

His wrath consumed him, boiling in every cell of his body. He was shaking, just like Randi used to. He longed to kill, to torture someone, to hear screams of pain, to see and smell blood.

With much effort, Po reminded himself that the game was not over yet. He could not kill Anna. He needed her and her magic. That was not the case for her man, though. The bastard was doomed. His destiny was sealed the very moment he touched Anna. Po would know who he was and would enjoy making him pay for everything.

Bending over the table like a voracious predator ready to strike, the main priest formulated yet another question. The bones rattled as they fell on the smooth wooden surface, forming the answer Po was seeking: "Raven".

THE WEDDING GIFT

Shortly after their wedding at the Star Gate, Anna sat in the small boat, opposite Raven. He was magnificent; his arm muscles rippled as he rowed, and a strand of fair hair fell on his face. He was smiling at her, and she felt lightheaded with happiness.

She reached out and tucked the fallen strand of hair behind his ear. He turned his head and placed a quick kiss on her hand.

Anna bit her lip, grinning.

Raven's eyes darkened, and he swallowed hard. "If you keep doing this, we will never get to the ship … but I won't regret it."

Anna laughed. It was unbelievable how much she felt at ease with him, given that she had met him only one day ago! She put her hand back on her lap.

"How did you get out of the castle for tonight?" she asked him, changing the subject. "If you slept there last night, then the queen expected you to stay tonight as well."

Raven nodded. "This is true. We came to negotiate a trade agreement. As a king, I am supposed to accept the queen's hospitality and sleep in the castle while we are here. However, I did not tell the queen that I have a twin brother. He is sleeping in the castle now, instead of me."

"Oh."

Sometimes, Anna wished she had a brother or a sister. She

had never thought what it would be like to have a twin until now, and her imagination soared.

"How kind of him," she marveled.

Raven grinned at her mesmerized expression. "Olaf is my best friend. He always has been. He has heard the prophecy, and he fears for me, but he agrees that I should spend as much time with you as I can."

"Thank him for me."

"I will, but you will soon meet him anyway."

When the boat neared Raven's ship, Anna turned on her seat to watch. It was so majestic it seemed unreal in the silvery moonlight. Anna reached out to touch its wooden side. The wood was cool and smooth under her fingers.

Two men kept watch. They came to help Anna get onboard and greeted her politely. Raven followed her. The men didn't speak Anna's language, so Raven translated for her. Speaking in whispers, so as not to wake the rest of the crew, he told her their names—Ottar and Helgi, and he explained to them that Anna was their new queen, for they had wed under the Star Gate.

Ottar and Helgi looked surprised, but their curious glances and smiles told Anna that they found her good enough for their king. They bowed to Anna and welcomed her as their new queen. A blush crept up Anna's cheeks, but Raven was beaming. He took her hand and led her to the center of the ship, where a small tent stood, protecting their provisions.

"Wait here," Raven told Anna and climbed into the tent.

She didn't have to wait long—he emerged, holding a small wooden box.

"What is it?" Anna asked.

Raven grinned. "Open it."

Anna did as he told her and gasped—inside was a necklace of exquisite beauty. Created by a skillful, loving hand, it curved elegantly, like a delicate plant, and tiny, star-shaped diamonds sparkled happily in every curve.

"Your wedding present," Raven whispered, his emerald eyes shining even brighter than the diamonds.

Anna felt breathless. Her eyes were suddenly wet with emotion. She wanted to say so many things but could not find the words to express how she felt. She had never seen such a fine jewel in her life, but the look on Raven's face, the love that shone in his eyes, was even more stunning. He was her man. She loved him with all her being, and he loved her, too.

"It's ... beautiful."

Raven took the necklace and carefully fastened it around Anna's neck. She stood motionless, enjoying his touch, her eyes feasting on him. She knew she could look at him forever and never get enough. He was her most precious gift. Anna rose on her tiptoes and brushed a kiss to his lips. His arms slid to her waist and he hugged her close.

"Why didn't you wake me up?" someone whispered nearby with pent-up annoyance.

Anna broke their kiss and turned. An older man stood next to them, his hands on his hips.

"Anna, this is Orm," Raven explained. "He is our source of wisdom and great tales."

Orm's eyes twinkled. He bowed slightly to Anna. "I am honored to finally meet you. Pray, tell me everything I have missed."

The corners of Raven's lips moved up in a badly hidden grin. "If we don't tell him, he will never leave us alone." Without breaking his hug, Raven told Orm about the wedding at the Star Gate.

The old man's eyes glistened excitedly. "So you remembered the legend I told you?" he muttered.

Raven nodded, "Of course. How could I ever forget?"

The wrinkles around Orm's eyes deepened as he smiled. "My congratulations to the both of you."

Orm stepped closer and gave Raven a fatherly hug. Anna could feel Raven meant a lot to him, and she felt a liking toward the old man.

Then Orm turned to Anna.

"Welcome, Anna, our new queen," he said affectionately, and hugged her as well.

"Thank you," Anna whispered, moved by his sincerity.

"May your life together be long and very happy," Orm wished, and Anna's heart skipped a beat—how much she wanted for his wish to come into being!

Meeting Raven's eyes, she knew he was thinking the same thing.

It was their night, and both Anna and Raven were determined to enjoy it to the fullest. It was easy to push sad thoughts away when they were together.

Raven showed her the ship, explaining the purpose of everything. Anna caught his every word, fascinated and delighted. Her reaction made Raven glow with pride. She asked questions about sailing, and Raven answered, never letting go of her hand.

When there was nothing left to explore, they sat on the stern, talking. They had so much to tell each other that a whole lifetime did not seem enough. Orm brought them some food—water, dry bread, and cheese—and they ate gratefully.

Anna told Raven about her life and about Nim, and Raven told her about his childhood and his parents.

"How did it feel to become a king at such a young age?"

Raven sighed. "I wish I could lie to you and tell you that it was like a dream suddenly coming to life, but I felt none of that. I never doubted that Olaf would be the next konungr, and I was perfectly fine with it. I didn't mind following a leader. When I realized that it was not a joke and I was being voted a konungr, I felt scared. We were at war, and I was supposed to win where my father had already failed... I am still marveling at how incredibly lucky I was then—me, a ten-year-old boy. By a lucky coincidence, I killed a grown man who was a king and a very good swordsman." Raven shook his head in disbelief. "I knew that my people's lives depended on me. I can still feel their stares on my back. I felt small and weak, and I did not want to fight, but I feared above all that I would not be able to protect them. A konungr's primary duty is to take care of his people, to make sure they are safe and well, even if he has to sacrifice his own life for it. Sometimes, I wish this responsibility were not mine."

Anna snuggled closer to him, and he kissed the top of her head.

"Did you ever want to become a queen?"

Anna shrugged. "When I was small, I used to pretend that I was a queen, like my mother. It only seemed appealing because of that. But after my last visit to the castle, I figured there is no reason for me to be queen—unlike Po, I do not crave power. Besides, I feel nothing for these people. I don't want to do anything for them, let alone make a sacrifice."

"Sorry, I just made you a queen of my people," Raven answered.

Anna looked up at him. A mischievous grin played on his lips.

She grinned back at him. "That's different. For you, I can do that. I will be happy to care for those who you love and for those who are important to you. Besides, your people are different. They did not let themselves get manipulated by power-hungry evil priests, and they will not betray you."

Raven shook his head. "People are the same everywhere. It's human nature. My people can also do stupid things, fall prey to manipulations, and betray the ones they love. It doesn't always mean they are evil. My duty is to protect them as best I can, sometimes even from themselves."

Anna caught his every word and nodded thoughtfully. "I know you are right. I don't feel this wisdom in my heart, but I will remember your words and try to act upon them."

A boyish grin spread over Raven's face. "You are perfect as you are, Anna. Your wisdom is different but just as precious."

Anna looked into his eyes and felt breathless. She loved his grin, she loved the way his eyes shone, the scent of him, the sound of his voice … and she craved his kiss.

He unmistakably understood what she was thinking about and covered her mouth with his. Anna's whole being answered as she kissed him back.

"So, you are a magician?" Raven asked her some time later.

"Aye. It's in my blood. Nim is my teacher."

"And magic is your best weapon?"

Anna shrugged. "Truth be told, I don't have a favorite weapon. I am quite good with a bow, and I can use daggers. Magic is what I use most because it is convenient, but my skills are not strong enough to match Nim's."

Raven's gaze was full of admiration. "I am not used to magic. I have never witnessed it, apart from the rune casting."

Anna's blue eyes sparkled mischievously. "You want me to show you?"

Raven nodded with badly hidden excitement.

Anna quickly considered her options and decided to go with the easiest thing. With a flicker of her hand, she produced a small flame that hung in the air in front of her. She made it stretch out and form a palm-sized flower, which floated over the waves in front of them, at a safe distance from the ship.

Raven was in awe. "Is it difficult to do?"

"Nay, this one is easy, but there are spells that are difficult. They require a lot of energy."

"Your energy?"

Anna nodded. "The energy of my body. It is exactly like any other physical effort, such as wielding a sword or running."

"What else can you do?"

"I can heal some wounds, place protections, talk to animals, brew potions, lift things in the air, open doors, find invisible traces of people, climb the walls without sliding. I can break things without touching them. I can also deflect spells."

Raven took her hand and placed a kiss on it. "You are amazing," he whispered.

Anna laughed. "*You* are amazing. What is your favorite weapon?"

"The sword. I inherited my father's sword, and I mostly fight with it. It is a fine weapon, and I cherish it because it was my father's."

"May I see it?"

"Aye." Raven unsheathed his sword and handed it to her.

Anna slowly slid her fingers over the blade and closed her hand around the hilt. "It is beautiful."

"You want to try and wield it?"

"Oh, nay," Anna laughed. "To give everyone a good laugh with my awkward attempts to lift it?"

Raven playfully rolled his eyes at her. "I'm sure you can lift it! You are underestimating your own strength."

Anna glanced toward Ottar and Helgi. "Possibly, but I'd rather not ruin their good opinion of me just yet."

They spent the rest of the night talking, avidly learning about each other, laughing, and savoring every moment.

When the sky started to turn gray, Raven took Anna back to the Star Gate. Leaving her on the rocky coast, he felt as if his heart was being torn apart.

He forced himself to push the boat back into the water and to row away. His very soul longed to be with her. If only he could take her and sail away with her right now, even before the town woke up! But he could not leave Olaf and a good dozen of his warriors here at Po's shady mercy, however tempting that may seem. Plunging the oars into the water with more strength than was needed, he was lost in thoughts. He had to decide what to do now.

Anna stood by the Star Gate, watching Raven's boat sail back to the ship in the dim light of the dawning day. Leaning on the cold stone archway that now kept their secret, she thought that she had just lived the best night of her life. She didn't want to let him go. She would have given anything to never come back and sail away with him anywhere, even to the very end of the world.

The main priest bent over the sleeping man, examining him attentively in the torchlight. There could be no doubt—it was Raven.

The room was constantly watched, and the guards would not lie to their master. Raven had come to the room in the evening and had been there ever since. At Po's order, a woman was sent to the treacherous king this night, and the bastard had gratefully accepted her—she was peacefully sleeping by his side, her hand resting on his chest.

Po's wrath and loathing were still boiling inside of him, and Raven was about to taste it all, but there was something that made the main priest hesitate: how could the wild Northman be in two different places at the same time? The bones did not lie. According to them, at this very moment, Raven was also with Anna. Did he manage to cheat on Anna this very night? That would be a very interesting turn of events that Po could use to his advantage.

Po rubbed his chin with a finger. Raven could not be a magician, but then what was his trick? The Northman was not that simple after all, but he was no match for the most powerful magician in the world. Somehow, this man had touched a very precious possession of Po's, and the main priest knew no forgiveness. From now on, the sleeping king was his prisoner. He didn't even know it yet, and it could be interesting to keep him blissfully unaware for some time.

The weak will always be my puppets, thought Po.

His wrath was under control now. After all, he had as much time as he wanted. He would find out Raven's secret, and he would make the man suffer as much as possible. There was no need to torture him right now—Raven was in his power, and from there, there was no escape. Ever.

 THE GHOST

Back home, Anna told Nim everything, savoring the sweet taste of her memories. Afterward, she went to bed, looking forward to the upcoming night. There was going to be a full moon, and Nim was getting ready to perform her rituals upon Po's dagger.

"Go to your captain," she told Anna. "I'll do it alone and tell you everything later. Who knows how much time you have left?"

Anna woke up in the evening and obediently swallowed her meal before running to her date.

She sat by the Star Gate with her back against the rough stone and waited, recalling every moment of their magical night.

The sun set, and darkness slowly enveloped the surroundings, but Raven's ship remained motionless.

Anna waited.

The full moon rose above the sea, huge and almost orange. There was still no sign of the boat.

Anna started worrying. She didn't doubt Raven's feelings for even a second—she felt his love deep inside her, for as she discovered, it was part of the ancient magic linking the two souls that were one before. She knew something kept him from coming, and as she had no way to find out what it was, anxiety kept growing inside her, enhanced by the still vivid memory of her last nightmare.

One candlemark, two—still nothing. A thick cloud slowly crept forward, partly covering the moon. The ship stood quiet, sleeping in the moonlight, just like the town and the glowing white castle.

At the fourth candlemark of waiting, Anna finally saw a dark spot in the sky. The raven! The bird silently soared down to her outstretched arm and locked his glance onto hers, taking her back to the castle.

Raven sat on his bed, fully dressed. He didn't talk, but with a slight movement of his head, he indicated the thick iron bars on the tiny window of his room. Then he broke the connection.

A cold shiver ran down Anna's spine—they held him captive!

"He is unharmed, but he is being watched," the bird told her, talking into her mind for the first time.

Frowning, Anna nodded. "I'll try to think of something. Please, go there and keep an eye on him. If you see anything useful, try to let me know," she begged. The raven croaked and took off. The bright full moon disappeared completely behind the cloud.

Anna started pacing nervously.

"Calm down and think clearly," she ordered herself. Thoughts were hard to gather, and panic stayed inside her, a tight knot forming in her belly. Anna tried to consider her options.

She could go to the ship and gather Raven's men to save him, but they would be only a handful against the queen's army, and Po was a dreadful magician. Otherwise, she could go to the castle alone. That would be even more stupid.

Anna took a steadying breath. She had to find Nim. Nim could always think clearly and would surely find a solution, but Nim was busy with her ritual. Anna didn't want to disturb her. She wouldn't call; she would go to Nim herself.

She mentally called her horse, twisting her bracelets. Soon, the clatter of hooves reached her.

Anna had already turned to leave when she thought she saw something. She halted, staring at the beach. Something was moving there. Dark shades, most likely people, gathered in small groups. They were getting into the boats.

Anna's palms were suddenly wet, and a panicked gasp broke from her lips. There could be no doubt—these people were about to attack Raven's ship! In a flash, Anna saw Orm's kind old face, and Ottar and Helgi, who smiled at her, other men whom she hadn't met yet, but who were Raven's loyal crew and friends. They were about to be attacked. Would they be able to fight off the attackers? Possibly, if no one used magic against them.

Anna's stomach clenched—Po wasn't one to fight fairly. For all she knew, Raven's crew could be tricked or even put to sleep.

Her heart hammering in her ears, Anna watched helplessly as the boats departed. They crept noiselessly toward the beautiful ship under the cover of darkness.

An awful sense of helplessness washed over Anna. She was several miles away. There was no way for her to reach them on time, and they were too far to hear her warning.

Twisting her hands in exasperation, she bit her lip so hard that she drew blood. Her brain raced in search of a solution. She had to do something!

The sour taste of her own blood suddenly brought forward a memory. Years ago, Nim had told her about a ritual. It was difficult and dangerous, and it required blood. Anna had never done it before, but lives were at stake, and she had to at least try to save them.

Her hands shaking, Anna drew out her knife and made a

deep cut on her palm. Then she picked up a stone with a more or less flat surface and drew a magical sign on it with her own blood. Steadying her breath as best she could, she pressed her bleeding palm to the stone and recited the incantation.

At first, she thought it hadn't worked, but then the world swirled around her. It moved faster and faster, until she felt unbearably dizzy. Squeezing her eyes shut, Anna tried not to throw up. All of a sudden, the swirling stopped. Anna carefully opened one eye, then the other. The world around her had turned black and white.

It was not the only surprise. Her own body lay motionless over the stone. She was contemplating it from aside. It worked! It was weird—she felt everything but her own body. She could hear and sense things like before, but she was light and transparent, like a ghost.

Meanwhile, treacherous boats were inching closer to Raven's ship, encircling her. They were dangerously near, but no one on the ship seemed to react.

Anna tried to move and found herself airborne. She couldn't walk or run, but the force of her mind could easily propel her forward. She quickly tried it, figuring out how it worked, and soon she was flying toward the ship faster than any bird.

She caught a glimpse of herself on the moving surface of the sea, and uttered an elated laugh. She was a pale bluish ghost, wearing the same gown that her physical body wore. If it weren't for her pale glow, she would have been invisible. She was glad to be visible, though—it would help her raise the alarm. If the men on the ship were still alive, that is.

Effortlessly, Anna reached the ship before the attackers. She halted over the deck. Raven's men lay here and there, wrapped in their cloaks. Loud snoring filled the air. One man had no cloak. He drove Anna's eye, for in Anna's black and white realm, his skin glowed pearly white. Anna realized with a start that he was dead. She looked around and spotted another pearly white man. They must have been keeping watch tonight.

She had to hurry. She badly needed to wake them.

Anna tried to shake the closest man, but her hands passed right through him. Her feelings were sharp in her new appearance—she could hear light splashes of the approaching boats, the whisper of the attackers' cloaks, and their light breathing.

Would the mere sight of her scare them enough to halt? Would they make enough noise to wake somebody?

She knew exactly when the attackers saw her—several of them drew a sharp breath. They halted but didn't make a sound.

Anna's mind raced. She couldn't touch them, but they must not know it for as long as possible.

Fixing her gaze at the closest man, Anna yelled at him to wake up. No sound came from her lips. From the corner of her eye, she saw one of the attackers silently gesturing to his companions. Panic raged inside of her. Please, nay! She could not fail! Not now, that she had come so far!

Exasperated, she mentally called to the man in front of her, the same way she talked to animals.

To her utmost surprise and relief, the man's eyelids shivered, and he slowly half looked at her. Then his eyes popped open with horror, his face turning ash-white.

Anna gestured toward the boats, articulating "ATTACK!"

The man just stared at her, petrified.

If Anna could feel her body, she would have squirmed with worry. Several boats had reached the ship by now, and one dark figure was already climbing onboard.

Anna turned away from the man she'd woken and moved toward the intruder. The man wore a long dark robe with a hood. A priest's robe. He met Anna's gaze, and his eyes widened with fear.

Fear. That was what she needed. Anna stretched her hands, as if she was about to catch him, slowly advancing on him.

The man instinctively recoiled and lost his balance. For a heartbeat, he struggled to regain it, but he quickly failed and fell into the water.

A loud splash tore the silence apart.

Relief washed over Anna as she watched Raven's men wake up. They were trained warriors—they were ready to fight instantly.

Their presence uncovered, the priests hurried onto the ship. Their long daggers glistened. The fight began.

Anna was determined to help. She moved alongside the ship, and everyone recoiled from her. It did not matter, as long as it helped Raven's men stay alive.

A man fell and a priest hurried to him, his dagger ready. Fast as lightning, Anna was there in a blink, floating above the fallen man. The priest hesitated, his dagger raised.

Now he would stab at her and find out that she was no danger to him.

But to her relief, someone came to their rescue—a sword plunged into the priest's back, the point coming out below his ribcage. The priest's eyes rolled, and his knees buckled.

Anna moved away.

Ottar pulled his sword from the flesh of the fallen enemy, while the fallen man sprang to his feet. He glanced at Anna and nodded. He knew she was their ally.

Anna moved along. Her vision blurred slightly, signaling that her strength was fading. She had to return to her body, but the fight was not over. She could not leave yet. Trying to ignore her weariness as best she could, she moved toward another priest.

And then she heard it. A faint brush and a hiss. The sound was too low for a human ear. Someone was starting a fire.

Anna felt a gush of fury. If anything, it gave her some strength.

She gestured toward the bow, hoping that someone would see it, and hurried there. Dark spots danced in front of her eyes. Moving overboard, she saw a priest in a boat. The magically conjured flames in his hands were already licking the wooden planks of the ship. Sensing that she had no more time left, Anna collapsed over the man, wishing her ghostly form would at least frighten him.

The last thing she saw was a flame, flickering close to her chest. Flattening darkness swallowed her.

THE BLOOD CONNECTION

Nim was kneeling in front of a large flat stone in the middle of a clearing. A round cavity on the stone's surface the size of a large plate, was filled with water. Its surface shivered slightly, the full moon reflected on it. The dagger and the wisp of Melaina's hair lay next to the pool.

Serene and relaxed, as if she were talking to an old friend about the weather, Nim was reciting complex spells. Her delicate fingers were slowly turning the dagger. Without stopping her recitation, she took one long black hair from the wisp. She carefully lowered it into the water, along with the dagger.

When both objects hit the bottom of the cavity, the water suddenly started boiling and bubbling, quickly changing colors. It lasted several heartbeats, but Nim just watched, undisturbed.

When the surface smoothed again, it was no longer transparent. A neat colored picture formed on it, and voices rang in the night, distinctive, as if they were real.

The old woman's blue gaze lit up with curiosity—she was about to see the last moments of Melaina's life.

Melaina rode away, leaving Anna with Nim. Bitter tears ran down her face, and her shoulders shook with sobs.

She halted her horse at the edge of the forest and stayed

there, forcing herself to calm down. Finally, she wiped away the tears and took several deep breaths.

"Stay calm and listen to what your heart tells you!" she said, repeating Nim's last words to herself. She flicked her hand, placing a protective shield around herself and her horse, and urged the animal forward.

The town bore painful traces of the rebellion—broken windows, blood stains, dead bodies, overthrown carts. Several houses were on fire, and people hectically ran around in abject chaos, mourning their dead or trying to save their scattered belongings.

Melaina urged her horse to a gallop. For the first time in her life, she was struggling not to look. She was there to save her husband.

The quickest way to the castle was blocked by dead bodies and makeshift barricades, and Melaina had to take small streets. It delayed her progress considerably—when she got to the castle, night had fallen already.

The star-shaped castle had been overtaken by the priests and their guards, but Melaina was not about to stop. Her protective shield firmly in place, she charged forward at a group of guards, oblivious to their arrows and swords.

The priests' guards were bewitched—they kept recklessly attacking her, not even noticing how useless their efforts were.

And again, Melaina willed herself to not intervene. One reckless man fell under the hooves of her horse and most likely died, but she did not halt, nor did she fight back. She had no time for that. She blew the gates open and hurried inside.

Screaming and cursing, the guards followed her. Melaina turned and cast a spell. Her pursuers slammed into an invisible barrier, their voices muffled. They would no longer be an issue.

Melaina dismounted and ran toward the closest door. The donjon looked empty. She checked it for any human presence with a spell, but no one was there. Melaina ran faster.

The next donjon was empty as well. Her footsteps echoed through the empty corridors. Was she too late? Her heart raced.

In the third donjon, four priests jumped at her. Melaina had no choice but to fight. True to herself, she did not fight to kill. Deflecting their spells, she masterfully stunned the first priest and bound together the other two. The fourth one was the shrewdest—he kept dodging and hiding, easily deflecting Melaina's spells. Twice he could have killed Melaina, yet he chose not to. Smashing furniture and blowing up vases, he was playing with Melaina, delaying her.

Melaina quickly understood his tactics. Her dark gaze sparkling with anger, she glanced around in search of a solution.

A statue flew past her, crashing on the large stone staircase that led to the lower level. Its broken pieces rolled and jumped, the sound magnified by the acoustics of the hall.

Melaina left her hiding place behind the corner and ran alongside the staircase.

The priest fired a spell at her. With a scream, Melaina fell on the stone floor.

Her strategy worked—the man did not want to kill her. He came closer and edged his hand close to Melaina's lips to check whether she was breathing.

Quick as a flash, Melaina sprang to life, biting his hand.

The priest cried in pain and surprise, but Melaina was ready. She caught the priest's arm with both hands and yanked him toward the staircase.

The man screamed as he lost his balance and fell headlong down the stairs.

Her chest heaving, Melaina stood up and ran.

The central donjon was also empty. She crossed the feast hall and ran across the corridors. It was dark there, but she did not slow down in the slightest. Jumping the stairs two at a time, she pushed open the door to the next donjon.

Voices were coming from the upper level. It was the donjon where the royal family lived. Melaina stopped and listened. Footfalls and talking. Muffled chanting. The knuckles of Melaina's hand on the door knob went white, her petrified gaze moving around hectically. Po was doing a ritual in her father's room. Suddenly, Melaina's free hand flew to her chest and she swayed on her feet. Her lips parted in a choked whisper "Ronen! Nay! Naaaay!"

Her face lost all color. Clutching her chest as if she had been stabbed, she slowly regained her balance and moved to go up but then changed her mind. Instead of facing Po's guards, she staggered downstairs. Ashen-faced and shaking, Melaina forced her feet to move faster, her breathing coming out in shaky gasps. Ice cold fear clouded her gaze.

She ran down a corridor and into a dark, empty room. She did not stop to light candles. She slid into the large fireplace and pushed on the stone wall. The wall moved away, and Melaina stepped into a pitch-black cramped passageway.

Painfully bumping her toes against the uneven steps, she hurried up, her quiet sobs betraying her internal agony.

The chanting grew closer, and Melaina moved faster. Her hands bumped into the door on the other side of the passageway, and she instantly blew it open.

The candlelight seemed too bright after the pitch-black darkness of the passageway, and Melaina squinted, her mind registering the sight nonetheless—the priests, in their white robes, stood in a circle around her father's bed, Po among them. They chanted incantations. Their chanting made Melaina shiver.

She blinked, forcing her eyes to adjust. Without stopping the incantation, Po looked at her, his gloating, violet gaze shining in triumph.

A blinding fury rose inside of her, turning her into a raging tornado. Melaina didn't think of a spell. She only moved her arm, willing for the priests to part, and the air exploded. Thrown several feet away from the bed, the priests crumpled like broken rag dolls.

Her arm still outstretched, Melaina stared at the bed. Her feet carried her forward without her being aware of it.

Ronen's feet and hands were tied to the bed. His face was frozen in a grimace of pain, his glassy eyes gazing at the skull-decorated hilt of the dagger protruding from his chest.

Melaina stood over Ronen's body. She looked paralyzed with terror, as if what she saw was too much to grasp. She slowly put her hand on Ronen's chest, her horror-stricken stare fixed on her husband's face.

On her left, Po slowly got to his feet.

"There is nothing you can do," he said. "It's over. His soul is dead."

He made a step toward Melaina.

As if awoken from her trance by his words, Melaina spun toward him, and her arm flew up.

The main priest was hurled against the wall. Still, he managed to raise a protective shield, which saved his life. A triumphant grin stretched across his thin lips.

Melaina's eyes narrowed. Her hand flicked again, and Po found himself trapped where he stood, as if locked in an invisible box.

Forgetting about him, Melaina turned to her husband's dead body. Her rage spent, she suddenly looked broken and miserable, her hair disheveled and her gown torn. Her shoulders fell, and tears rolled down her cheeks.

She slowly bent down and placed a tender, loving kiss on Ronen's lips. He must have died only a short time ago, for his lips were still red.

Melaina's hand slid down his chest and bumped into the dagger. She pulled away from him, blinking rapidly. Ronen's blood was on her fingers.

For a couple of heartbeats, Melaina stared at it. Then a sob broke from her lips, and her other hand closed around the hilt of the dagger. She pulled, and the weapon came free, blood dripping from its point.

Melaina caught the drop of blood with her hand and brought the dagger down, cutting her palm. Ronen's blood melted with hers, and her eyes widened. She blinked and tilted her head, looking at something visible only to her.

"Ronen," she breathed and made another deep cut on her palm.

She placed her bleeding hand over her husband's chest and clenched her fist. Blood oozed, dripping onto Ronen's wound.

Melaina hiccupped a sobbing laugh.

"Ronen, my love, I am coming!" she whispered. "I am here ..."

She straightened her back and lifted her chin. A smile lit her tear-stricken face. She took the dagger with both hands and, in one swift strike, plunged it into her heart.

Her eyes widened in shock, and she swayed, life quickly fading from her body. With an ultimate effort, she pulled the dagger free and collapsed on top of Ronen, her wounded heart over his.

"NAAAAAY!" Po cried out, his exasperated, blood-chilling cry echoing throughout the castle ground.

Melaina could no longer hear it, though—a serene smile played on her lips, her eyes lovingly staring into Ronen's.

When Melaina died, her blocking spell lifted, and Po ran to her. He flipped her to her back, hopelessly trying to bring her back to life, crying and begging and cursing the entire time.

Melaina was gone, and so was Ronen. She did save him—the grimace of pain was gone, and a light, blissful smile played over his dead face.

The vision ended. The reflection of the full moon was shivering on the surface of the water, the dark shape of the dagger glistening at the bottom of the cavity.

Nim sat motionless, thinking. She recognized the incantation that the priests were chanting. Po was mistaken—this particular spell, even if the priests had finished it properly, could not destroy a soul, but only trap it between life and death. Melaina had been smart and courageous. She used the blood connection, a magical phenomenon that was possible between the two parts of a soul, to communicate with Ronen and free him from the terrible fate Po had intended for him. She was happy to die, for she had departed together with her soul mate.

Worry tugged at Nim's insides—with Melaina's story now fully revealed, the prophecy about Anna's true love being doomed suddenly appeared in a new light. Nim suppressed a shiver, recalling Po's face, distorted with rage and pain. The man was mad and dangerous; he knew no mercy. Melaina did what he hated most—she rejected him, and that was something he would never forgive, or forget.

Now he certainly thought that Melaina had come back as Anna, and Anna was in grave danger. And as soon as he found out about Raven, Raven would be in danger as well. Po had almost twenty years to practice and correct his mistakes.

There was a good chance that he would want to succeed where he'd failed the last time. What if he had learned the right incantation? Nim's heart clenched at this thought.

Her hands shaking slightly, she retrieved the dagger and the hair from the water. Bending over the pool, she started reciting a different incantation. The past didn't bother her anymore. What really mattered was the future, Anna's future, and in order to make it a little less unbearable, she needed some urgent answers.

Two Parts of a Soul

ELENA'S REQUEST

Raven paced impatiently in his cell. It was the same room he had been given from the beginning, with the same furniture, and even with several plates of fresh food and drinks. Now, however, thick iron bars locked the small window, and a strange invisible wall separated him from the door. He was still surprised at how quickly they had turned his room into a prison cell. He had never dealt with magic before and found it extremely irritating, shrewd, and unfair. He felt completely helpless in front of it, and it frightened him. Unable to count on his physical strength anymore, Raven relied only on his instincts. They were not of much use either, despite the fact that he knew he was being watched constantly.

From the beginning of his rule and his first victory over the Foreigners, Raven had done his best to maintain unity and prosperity in his lands. He had organized educational expeditions and strengthened trade. He made sure all the men were trained to fight, but tried to avoid wars as much as possible, privileging negotiations and alliances.

Raven's quiet, prosperous lands attracted conquest-hungry neighbors like magnets. Moreover, the peace agreement that he had made with the Foreigners ended almost two years ago. He knew that the Foreigners were plotting a war against him, waiting for the right moment to strike.

Raven had several small allies, but it was not enough. He was known to be reckless, but only when it came to risking his own life. The lives of his people were very important to him. Before entering any war or battle, he carefully weighed all the chances and possibilities. The Vikings firmly believed death on the battlefield to be the most honorable for a man, but so far, Raven's decisions had given no reason for discontent. Most of his people loved him.

Raven wanted to avoid the war. It was for that precise reason he had come to see Queen Elena.

Separated by the sea, Elena's kingdom was bigger and much more powerful than Raven's. They hadn't been at war for years, for they were feared, and their army was of an enormous size.

Raven was no fool to hope that Elena would accept an alliance, for she had no interest in helping smaller kingdoms, but her kingdom could benefit from trade. Her lands were abundantly covered with fine wood, which Raven needed to build more ships. The fleet was his major advantage—their ships were faster and lighter than the ships of their enemy. Raven had personally tested that out on numerous occasions.

The enemy was aware of this advantage. If he judged Raven's fleet too powerful, he might refrain from attacking. Should he decide to attack nonetheless, Raven would have a real chance to win.

Raven wanted a trade agreement that would benefit both him and Elena, and hopefully, also prevent the queen from allying herself with his enemies.

He had come with honest and clear intentions, and his plan seemed quite easy to accomplish. From the moment he saw this land from the sea, though, he couldn't suppress the feeling that it would not go as planned, that it would not be easy. And the way he had been greeted left no doubt about that.

Then Anna had appeared, and his life changed. When he

first kissed her, he knew that he no longer cared about wood or alliances. He only wanted to end it and sail away with Anna as quickly as possible, for despite the apparent calm, he felt danger lurking nearby.

After he left Anna at the Star Gate, he'd hurried to the castle to take Olaf's place. To avoid any suspicion, Raven had to sneak in disguised as one of his men, who had brought additional gifts for the queen.

Olaf managed to leave the castle safely with two of Raven's men. Only their uncle, Sveinn, and Orm stayed to accompany Raven to Elena's midday meal.

Raven's intention was to quickly finish things with the queen and depart—that very evening, if possible. Then he would return to the Star Gate at night to take Anna with them, if everything went as planned.

To his relief, it seemed that Elena finally decided to get to business—even before the meal, she finally announced that she was ready to listen to them, adding that even though she enjoyed their company, a good queen had to place her people's interests first.

Raven did not take offense, complimenting her devotion to her people, which doubtlessly was the reason for the glory and prosperity of her lands. Not that he really meant it—he understood that the kingdom was in slow recession and Elena was but a capricious puppet of her own main priest. None of the showy ceremonies they'd organized could fool him, but he was not there to advise her on her internal politics, so he contented himself with simply observing and playing her game.

The room where Elena brought them was spacious and brightly lit. A long wooden table stood in the middle with tall, cushioned chairs around it.

Po and three other priests were already there, politely waiting for everyone to take a seat.

Queen Elena sat at the head of the table. There was no chair opposite her. She gestured for Raven and his men to sit on her right, while Po and his priests took a seat on the left of her.

Raven found himself across from Po.

"Interesting," he thought, *"is that Po's way of showing who is really making the decisions here?"*

His expression neutral, he shifted his chair slightly, a half turn toward the queen. He then leaned back and put his hands in front of him in an open, non-threatening gesture. Observing Po out of the corner of his eye, he politely waited for the queen to begin.

The main priest looked perfectly impassive. He leaned back on his chair as well, his arms folded over his chest.

Communication was a complex process in this kingdom. Raven knew it and was very careful. He was determined to stay polite, no matter how they provoked him. He knew he could count on Orm, Sveinn, and his uncle to stay controlled as well. He had chosen them purposefully—they could restrain their pride and wouldn't intervene unless he needed them to.

"King Raven," Elena started in a low, sensual voice, "what is the reason for your visit? Pray, tell me everything. I'm impatient to hear what favors you hope to get from a woman like me."

"Oh…"

Raven had noticed that everyone in Elena's castle spoke this way. It was a manner of speaking, not an attempt to flirt, but Raven found it repulsive. However, he remained impassive. His body would not betray him—his pupils and his heartbeat did not change in the slightest, for he shared his mind with his raven and was able to transfer all his emotions to the bird.

Po didn't betray his feelings either, but Raven felt that the priest was observing him closely, as if he were on high alert for the slightest reaction.

"I am not seeking a favor," Raven answered calmly. "I am looking for an opportunity that would benefit both your people and mine. You have wine, wood, and spices. We have walrus ivory, furs, stones, metals, jewelry, and other things that we are willing to trade for it. You are a wise and visionary queen, from what I have heard. You can certainly see the positive outcome it would mean."

Disappointment showed on Elena's face, and her red brows creased in a frown.

Apart from her cheekbones, there was nothing in this woman that reminded him of Anna, despite the fact that Elena was a second cousin of Anna's. Amused, he pictured Elena's expression if Anna were to come here and tell her who she really was. Thinking of Anna warmed his insides. How fortunate that his thoughts had no impact on his own physical body! Still, it was not the right moment to dwell on all the sweet memories he shared with Anna, for he had to stay alert, to be in the present moment.

"And what do you need the wood for, if you don't mind me asking?" Po suddenly said, interrupting Elena, who was about to say something.

Perfectly calm, Raven turned to him. The real game was about to start. Whether they accept his offer or not, he wanted it to be over quickly. He decided to go with the truth. He had a feeling that Po already knew the answer anyway and had his strategy planned around it.

"We need it to build ships."

"So King Raven is increasing his fleet ..." the main priest mused, his stare full of implication.

Raven instantly understood what this game was about. So

be it. His only wish now was to leave as soon as possible and to take Anna with him.

He shrugged. "Aye, I am. My neighbor, king Coenred, is planning a war against me, and I must be ready to deflect his attack."

"King Coenred?" Elena blinked incredulously. "I thought he was entirely focused on going south …"

"Maybe King Raven simply wants to attack King Coenred first," Po suggested carefully. "After all, people from the North are known for their liking of bloodshed."

Once again, Raven didn't react. The stakes were much higher than his pride, and no flattery or insult would ever determine what his people were worth. He bluntly brought the discussion back to what interested him.

"So what do you think? Would you agree to trade with my people?"

Raven could tell it was not the right thing to say—Po rolled his eyes at him. "Oh! You are so impatient! Forgive me, King Raven, but it makes me believe that you have not told us everything …"

When Raven remained impassive, he went on, "Let's say we agree to your terms. How can Queen Elena be sure that you are not planning an attack on her? To destroy us with our own wood?"

Raven sighed inwardly. This was starting to get on his nerves.

"My dear friend," he answered calmly, "I am not a conqueror, and I have never been in a war to conquer, but I will not allow anyone to take our lands from my people. However, to make you feel safe, Queen Elena, I am willing to make a peace treaty with you as well."

"A peace treaty …" Po uttered, nodding thoughtfully.

"Aye." Raven met the queen's watery gaze. "It will guarantee that I will not attack you, if you doubt the fact that I have no interest in attacking your lands."

The queen averted her gaze and pouted.

Raven could not figure out what was wrong with her, so he decided to simply ignore it.

"A peace treaty could be beneficial for both your people and mine. I am ready to sign it with you right now, if you wish."

Po's gaze also turned to Elena. His posture did not change, but Raven sensed his tension.

Raven's body was relaxed, but all of his senses were ablaze. He instinctively felt danger, even though he could not find any reason for it, no matter how hard he tried.

Elena did not look at him as he spoke, her blank gaze focused on her own marble-white hands, but then her lashes shivered, and she shyly met his gaze.

"I thought …" she started pathetically, red stains slowly appearing on her snow-white cheeks, "I hoped that you were more considerate than that, King Raven." Anger and disappointment were mixed into her expression. "I'm but a young woman, and the destiny of all this kingdom is resting upon my shoulders. I have to bear this responsibility alone. Can you imagine how many times men have tried to deceive or manipulate me?"

"Aye, and it looks like they are still very successful at it."

Raven almost raised a brow in surprise. Was she expecting him to play her rescuer? Raven was sure Elena's words and behavior were part of Po's game. He couldn't help thinking of how different things would have been if Anna were queen instead of Elena. Anna would never have fallen prey to the priest's manipulations.

Elena hadn't finished her speech yet. She bent toward Raven and put her hand on his forearm, speaking so passionately that for a while, Raven believed there might be a bit of truth in it.

"You seem to me a man of honor, and I've heard a lot of your strength and wisdom. And if you really care about the future of our people, as you say you do, let us unite our lands through wedding! We will form a big and powerful kingdom that no one will dare attack. You will have your wood, as much as you need to build your ships, without stupid agreements. You will have my people for your army and me to warm your bed every night. And I will ..." her voice quivered slightly. She looked away and finished in a shy whisper, "I will have a strong, wise husband to protect me and give me beautiful and healthy children."

Raven was surprised. He had expected anything but that, yet his expression remained unfathomable and calm as he weighed every word of his answer.

Elena's hand clenched on his forearm, and she met his gaze. Her face was scarlet, and her eyes shone madly, their pupils abnormally dilated against her watery-gray irises.

"I love you, Raven," she begged, a hysterical edge echoing in her voice, "and I really need you. Be a man and assume your king's duty!"

Raven listened to her with a mixture of pity and disgust. He refrained from shaking her sweaty hand off his forearm only because the raven was still taking all of his emotions. Elena looked disturbed, mad. Something was wrong with her eyes, her pupils being much bigger than normal. Was it drugs? The almost hysterical passion of her words contrasted brutally with her previous coldness and detachment. She was talking about love, but it sounded distorted and even scary coming from her. It was hard to imagine Elena loving anyone, including him. He sensed that she felt nothing for him just as sure as he felt Anna's love, which was always there, at the very core of his being, warming and strong.

His gaze unwavering, Raven slightly bowed his head and answered in a calm, even voice. "Thank you, Queen Elena. Thank you from the depths of my heart for your feelings toward me, and for believing me better than I really am. I deeply admire your devotion to your people and your inner strength. Your offer is very wise and tempting, but I will not become one of those evil men who seek to deceive you. I cannot accept it, for I am already married."

Surprise briefly crossed Po's expression.

"But no woman is waiting for you in your town," Po stated, his piercing gaze scrutinizing Raven's expression.

Again, Raven decided to go with the truth. "True. She hasn't arrived to my town yet, but she's on her way."

Finally, Queen Elena caught the meaning of what Raven had just told her. Her face twisted with rage, and her watery eyes narrowed threateningly, "Oh, really? Pray, tell me who she is! Is her kingdom bigger and stronger than mine? I've never heard of someone like that!"

Raven calmly shook his head. "Nay. Her kingdom is very small, but I am wed to her, and there is no going back."

Elena's eyes filled with tears of rage, but it was not her who worried Raven the most—across from him, the main priest leaned back in his chair. His expression was unfathomable, but something made Raven think of a snake about to strike.

Raven could not know that from the moment his last words left his lips, his future was sealed. The irreversible count had started; the prophecy was turning into reality. At that precise moment, however, only one person knew about it. Only one person, whose decision had just been made. Only one person, who could not even imagine then how many lives it would affect, or the long trail of pain and suffering it would leave in its wake.

"You are selfish and stupid!" hissed Elena. "A good king must sacrifice himself for the good of his people, no matter what his heart desires! And there is no better queen for your people than me, do you hear?"

Grateful beyond measure for his bond with the bird, Raven remained calm and controlled as he respectfully bowed his head to Elena. "You are absolutely right. I'm but a weak common man, who is not worth someone like you. I deeply admire you, Queen Elena, but I have said my vow, and despite my weaknesses, I cannot break it."

His words seemed to madden Elena even more.

"So be it!" she shrieked. "There won't be any agreement between us! And from now on, you are my enemy!"

She stood so quickly that her chair fell on the floor with a crash, but she did not seem to notice.

All the men hurried to stand up as well, following the rules of etiquette.

Raven knew they had to leave now. The ship was ready—the raven was already warning Olaf, and then he would warn Anna.

Raven bowed to Elena with respect. "I came here with peace in my heart, Queen Elena, and I told you the truth. Thank you for your hospitality."

His men bowed too, the same polite expression on their faces.

But the queen issued a high, hysterical laugh. "You aren't going anywhere, King Raven! *I* am the queen here! From now on, you are my enemy, and you will be treated as such!"

Raven glanced at his men. They moved closer, ready to defend themselves.

Then everything happened so fast that none of them could do anything to resist. Po's hand flickered, and heavy ropes appeared out of nowhere, swishing and twisting in the air like snakes. In a heartbeat, Raven, Orm, Örjan, and Sveinn were bound from head to toe, struggling for air, their swords lying helplessly on the floor next to them.

Po laughed at their bewildered expressions—a low, cruel laugh, as mad as Elena's.

"Did you really think that your swords could match us?" he asked, bending over Raven.

Raven wanted to retort, but he could not breathe, his chest squeezed too tightly by the ropes. He could only stare back.

"You are pitifully helpless in front of magic, King Raven. Your people are still too primitive to learn it," the main priest crooned, trying to humiliate him as much as he could.

Raven frowned, and Po laughed again. "To prove that to you, King Raven, I will even leave you your sword in your cell!"

The prisoners were magically lifted into the air, and Raven saw his own fear reflected in his friends' eyes before they were separated.

OLD NIM

Po kept his word. Raven was brought back to his room, which stayed the same, apart from the thick iron bars that appeared on the only window.

The priest who brought him removed his ropes with a flick of his hand. Raven instantly sprang to his feet and leaped toward him, but he slammed painfully into an invisible wall. The priest stood by the door, gloating, and Raven stopped. He would explore the magical barrier later. Soon, the priest was gone.

Raven carefully examined his room. The invisible barrier stood tall and unbreakable—from wall to wall, and from the ceiling to the floor. The iron bars on the window were also real and solid. Running his hand over them, Raven could not believe the way they had magically appeared in but a motion of a hand. Perhaps the bars had been there all along, magically hidden from view. Through the window, he could see one of the castle gardens. No one seemed to be there, but Raven sensed he was being watched.

Raven searched the walls and checked every stone on the floor, but there was no way out.

The sun set, and a priest brought him some food and water. He made the tray float in the air toward Raven, careful to stay out of Raven's reach.

Raven did not move. He watched the tray soar through the invisible barrier and carefully land on the table, trying to figure

Two Parts of a Soul

out how it worked. He strained his brain, recalling everything he had heard about magic. He should have asked Anna more about it. What if the priest had to lower the invisible barrier for the tray to pass? It would be risky, for it would leave the priest exposed for some time. Still, it was a possibility, and Raven had to test it. Next time, then.

Without speaking a word to him, the priest was gone.

Raven did not touch the food. He did not trust them. Of course, they have already had multiple opportunities to kill him, even without using food or water, but they could have added something to weaken or drug him. Raven had only his physical strength against Po, and he could not risk losing it like that.

Restlessly thinking of his disastrous situation, he could not find a way out, and his intuition and the bird were now his only allies. He did not know whether the priests had somehow found out about his connection with the raven, so he decided not to take chances. At night, he briefly contacted Anna and Olaf, and then had a quick glimpse of the donjon where Orm, Sveinn, and Örjan were being kept. After that, he shut his mind down.

Po came the next morning with the priest who had brought him food. He asked whether Raven had changed his mind. Raven only laughed in response. Po was not particularly pleased by that, but he said nothing and left.

The day went just like that—nothing was happening, and time dragged on. Raven was hungry and thirsty, and his helplessness increasingly irritated him.

He felt tired but fought off the sleep that threatened to engulf him—sleeping was dangerous, especially when he was being watched. Raven was a trained warrior and knew that he could go without food and sleep for several days. He paced in the room, trying to think of a solution. Sometimes he checked the magical wall and the bars on the window, but they remained in place, firm and solid, giving him no possibility of escape.

Night fell, but nothing changed. Tired and irritated, Raven sat on the bed. He did not notice a hand that placed a small bowl with some brew on his window. A delicate, barely perceptible smell wafted into the room, and before he knew it, Raven had dozed off.

It was Raven's instinct that woke him, for the silence around him remained undisturbed. His eyes were closed, but he could clearly sense someone's presence next to him. Blaming himself for dozing off, he half opened one eye.

A tiny, fairy-like woman with shining golden hair stood in front of him. She was thoughtfully observing him, her head tilted slightly.

His first thought was that he was dreaming or hallucinating. He shook his head and blinked. The vision did not vanish. The woman was really there. Though his mind was slowed by the potion, he recognized her nonetheless.

"Nim? How did you get here?"

A light smile touched the woman's lips, and her blue eyes sparkled. "So Anna told you about me …"

Raven smiled and shrugged. "You are her only family."

Nim's eyes shone with affection.

"You are as handsome as she described …" she stated, and then she began to speak more urgently. "Time is scarce. Get up, warrior, and gather your belongings. We are leaving."

Raven stood up. He felt a little dizzy.

Nim must have known how he felt—she offered him a flask.

"It will make you feel better."

Raven took the flask from her. It smelled like herbal tea. Raven was not sure whether he liked Nim, but she was Anna's family, so he decided to trust her. He took a big gulp. The taste was not bad, and his mind began to clear.

"Keep the flask. Let's go." Nim said firmly and walked to the door. The invisible wall was gone.

"My warriors are imprisoned in the opposite donjon," Raven whispered. "I want to free them."

The fairy woman looked up at him. She seemed even smaller next to him, barely reaching his waist.

"Another reason to hurry."

Nim pushed the door open, and they stepped into the dark archway, where just a couple of days before, he had caught Anna. Alert for any presence, they hurried into the darkness outside. Nim broke into a run, and Raven fell into step with her.

"I think someone was spying on me back in the cell," he whispered to her.

Without stopping, the tiny woman nodded. "Was ..." She ran quickly and noiselessly, with surprising grace and ease. Showing her the way to the donjon where his men were held captive, Raven couldn't help asking, "Nim, are you by any chance from—"

She did not let him finish. "There's no time for it."

Örjan, Orm, and Sveinn were locked in a real prison cell with a tiny window at the level of the ground. They were given much less comfort than their chieftain.

"Tell them to move back from this wall," whispered Nim, indicating the small window with an impatient wave of her hand.

Raven did not like being ordered around, but Nim was their savior and Anna loved her. Besides, she was older, so Raven swallowed his irritation and crouched by the small window, talking to his men in whispers.

"Now move back," Nim said behind him.

Raven did not have time to rise from his crouch as Nim stretched out her hand. She did not make a sound, and her face did not move, but the entire wall with the tiny window vanished without a noise, a gaping black hole left in its stead.

The woman looked at her work with silent satisfaction and lowered her hand. "They may get out now."

Quick and silent, Orm, Sveinn, and Örjan climbed out, glancing at Nim with fear and awe.

Nim gestured toward the front of the castle.

"Get the horses and leave silently," she instructed them. "I opened the main gate for you." Then she looked at Raven. "Take Anna and run away with her. As far as you can. Hurry!"

"Where is Anna?"

Nim frowned. "I have no time to find that out. Does she know you were caught?"

Raven nodded, looking at her expectantly.

"Sooner or later, she will come home looking for me," the woman concluded with conviction. "Ride to the forest and leave your horse at the edge." She thrust a pine needle into his hand. "Here. Put it on your palm, and it will point you in the right direction."

Raven bowed to Nim. "Thank you for your help, Nim. I will never forget it."

She waved her hand. "Don't thank me, warrior. I would have killed you for taking Anna from me, but that would only serve to hurt her. Go, and tell Anna not to worry about me!"

With that, she turned on her heels and hurried back toward the castle.

Raven nodded. It was not a very pleasant thing to know, but the piercing honesty of her words made him respect her even more.

He turned on his heels and ran in the opposite direction, following his men to the stables.

Anna awoke with a jolt. She was lying over the cold, hard stone, and her body felt sore and heavy. The sun had already disappeared behind the horizon, and the light was fading.

She struggled to her feet. Every movement was painful, and her skull was bursting with pain. Recalling the last events, she peered from behind the archway at the ship.

It wasn't there. Anna rubbed her eyes with her fists, but nothing changed. The ship was gone. The beach looked empty and motionless, and the sea was that mysterious dark blue that can only be seen right before the darkness.

Feeling weak and dizzy, Anna leaned on the archway and closed her eyes. What happened? How long had she been unconscious? The picture of Raven imprisoned in the castle stood out clearly in her mind. Anna blinked her eyes open and looked around in a desperate hope to see the raven somewhere, but only seagulls soared above her, filling the air with their piercing cries. She heaved a sigh. Her magical sign was still visible on the flat surface of the stone. The dried blood had turned brown, and Anna's hand was still covered in it, so the fight on the ship did happen. But where was the ship now?

Questions throbbed inside her aching brain, but she had no strength to do anything whatsoever.

Fortunately, her horse was not far. The clever animal waited patiently for her mistress to mount and then trotted home, moving carefully to avoid causing Anna even more pain.

Resting her dull head against the horse's warm neck, Anna thought that Nim had been right when she warned her against those spells. But then again, Nim was always right. Tired even of thinking, Anna closed her eyes, completely trusting the animal. Soon, she dozed off.

She woke up because her horse neighed gently, informing her that they had arrived home.

It was already night. Groaning, Anna forced herself to slide away from the saddle. Her hand bumped against the flask of water in the saddle pocket. She pulled it out and drank. Cold, fresh water was like an elixir of life. The headache eased, and she felt much better.

Staggering slightly, she walked to the house and pushed the door open. It was dark inside, and she stepped in, too tired to check the house for any intruder.

Suddenly, strong arms closed around her. Anna gasped and lost her balance, falling against the familiar muscled chest.

"Anna!"

The dear, low voice sent a shiver down her spine. She hid her face in his chest, breathing in his unique scent.

"Raven!" she whispered. "Raven!"

"Nim freed us," he explained, lighting a candle with one hand and hugging Anna's shoulders with the other. "She says we must run away. She asks you not to worry about her."

Anna looked up at him. He was serious and focused, as if getting ready for a fight. Then he saw the traces of blood on her cheek, and worry crossed his beautiful face. "Are you wounded?"

Anna shook her head and quickly told him about the ship.

"I am so sorry! I blacked out before the fight ended."

Raven brought her closer and placed a kiss on top of her head.

"Don't worry," he whispered. "They are fine. The ship can sail and is already waiting for us."

Anna sighed with relief, thankful beyond measure for the ship's escape. She felt so good with Raven's strong arms wrapped around her that she did not want to move.

Raven cupped her face in his warm hands and looked into her eyes. "Anna, will you sail away with me?"

She didn't have to think. She didn't even pause to catch her breath. The answer was apparent to her from the moment their eyes had met for the first time. "I will follow you to the end of the world and beyond!"

He gave her that grin she loved so much, love shining in his emerald eyes.

They left the hut together. Anna's horse was waiting for them, moving her ears happily. They mounted and rode away from the wooden hut, which one of them would never see again.

Kateryna Kei

When Strength Becomes Weakness

They rode to the Star Gate. A boat would wait for them there to take them farther north to the ship. While the horse galloped forward, Raven told Anna everything that had happened in the castle.

As they rode, the night enveloped them in darkness. Heavy clouds hid the stars, and the air stood threateningly motionless and charged, like before a storm. The clatter of hoofs seemed excessively loud in the surrounding silence. No one pursued them, but Raven had a feeling that they were being watched. He did not tell Anna about it, as he was unwilling to worry her. They had to try. The stakes were bigger than ever before; both of them knew that living without each other would be the worst torture, for they had now experienced what it was like to share a soul.

Hurrying forward toward their destiny, they clung to each other like two children in the middle of a dark forest. They both sensed the approaching danger and, getting ready to face it, they savored the feeling of each other's touch and presence. It was like breathing; too good and never enough, and they were enjoying it, knowing that every breath could be their last.

The ride seemed too long and too short at the same time. When Raven finished his tale, they fell silent, tightly hugging each other and warily scrutinizing the surroundings for any sign of danger. The only sounds disturbing the sticky silence were the clatter of the hoofs, their breathing, and their heartbeats. No bird or animal was heard. The world seemed frozen in anxious anticipation.

Finally, the Star Gate appeared in front of them. The old archway stood silent and dark, its shadowy shape indistinct in the blackness of night. Below, someone was waiting for them in the small boat that floated on the black water. The figure was motionless, too. Too motionless.

The sense of foreboding increased. Something ominous was floating in the air, dark and cold, enveloping everything like sticky fog. The horse shivered and halted. Their nerves ablaze, Anna and Raven peered around them. Nothing moved. Anna muttered a spell to detect any human presence, but it showed none.

Raven met her gaze. His eyes shone with determination. Anna's heart responded with so much love that she reached up and quickly pressed her lips to his.

Surprised, he blinked at her and smiled, and then urged the horse forward. The mare shivered with all her body, her ears pressed to her head, but Raven persisted, and the horse abided, suddenly rushing down to the water, as if running from death itself.

Unknown danger lurked in the darkness around them. They instinctively felt it but could not see it. Dread and anxious anticipation unpleasantly tickled their nerves, waking the sickening fear in their stomachs.

The horse halted by the water.

Nothing happened.

The riders peered into the darkness. Rocks stood motionless around them. In the dark, they looked like mystical creatures with hole-like eyes. The figure in the boat still didn't move.

Anna took Raven's hand and dismounted. The black

silence around them was so thick that every breath seemed too loud. Shivering unwillingly, Anna turned her back to the horse and looked around, still holding Raven's hand.

All was quiet.

She had a bad feeling about it, and it was only getting worse. The hairs stood up on the back of her neck, and her heart hammered inside her chest.

Raven moved, dismounting as well, and the leather strap brushed her fingers. Anna recognized the bracelet with her magical sign.

It was the mixture of instinct and panic that made her do it. She moved her hand over Raven's, making her magical sign slide between their clasped palms, and whispered a protective spell.

Raven's feet touched the ground when the last sound left her lips, and the air exploded around them with blinding flashes of red light.

The horse neighed madly and fell dead. Anna screamed and grasped Raven's hand with both of hers to keep him as close to her as possible. Her worries were vain—the protective spell worked perfectly, shielding both of them. Like an invisible wall, the shield stood firm around them, turning deadly spells into bright red sparks as they hit it.

The figure in the boat was rowing toward them.

"Don't let go of my hand, no matter what!" Anna whispered. She stared unblinkingly at the figure. She knew who it was.

Raven knew he had to stay close to her. As much as she wanted to protect him, he was determined to protect her at any price. Adjusting his grip on her hand, he turned around, his back against hers, and unsheathed his sword.

Dark, hooded figures were silently emerging from behind the black rocks, mercilessly encircling them.

They were trapped.

The priests slowly gathered around them like jackals, not daring to come too close. Raven counted thirty-two of them, all armed with their long daggers and shields, and wearing long black robes.

Meanwhile, the boat arrived, and the man stepped ashore.

"Well, well, well …" he said and lowered his hood. His perfectly shaven skull looked even whiter in the darkness.

"Any use of magic is prohibited, and the punishment is death," Po announced casually, a gloating expression in his violet eyes.

Anna did not move, but instead stared intently at him, the red glow of the sparks reflected in her eyes. The warmth of Raven's back against hers was reassuring. She felt calm and ready to fight for her love and happiness.

"So that's your newly proclaimed wife, King Raven?" Po shook his head with disbelief, like a teacher telling off his disobedient students. "How disappointing of you! To fall under the charms of a poor little witch, forgetting about the well-being of your people! I thought you were stronger and wiser than that!"

Raven chuckled in response. "Apparently, I am not the only one stupid and weak here—you are in love with Anna as well, but with no success. As for my people, they will live better without your intervention."

Po's face went slightly red, making Anna roll her eyes in amazement—somehow, she could not imagine Po being in love.

The priests exchanged wondering looks, which made Po angry.

"Remove your protection, witch!" he ordered coldly. "You are both arrested!"

Anna did not react. She tightened her grip on Raven's

hand, wishing to be able to get through his skin and to protect him from the inside. He squeezed her fingers reassuringly, and she imagined that grin of his when she'd told him that she would follow him to the end of the world. They were together, and that was all that mattered. Whether they lived or died, they must remain together. She grinned.

"I said remove your protection!" repeated Po, even more irritated by her grin.

"Why would I listen to you? You killed the last king and my parents!" she answered, her voice clear and disdainful.

Po raised his eyebrows, and a sneer twisted his thin lips. "For your information, they deserved much more than what they got. And be reassured, I learned from my mistakes. I only wonder: how did *you* find out?"

His piercing stare searched her face for the confirmation of the answer he already knew.

Anna shrugged, feeling bold. "The same way you hid it from me."

Po nodded, entertained. "I like talking to you. Your temper makes me want to renew the experience ..." Then his face turned serious again and he said coldly, "Remove your protection or I will make you do it."

Anna shook her head fiercely.

He uttered a cold laugh. "Your resistance is stupid," he informed her. "You know that I'm much stronger and more experienced than you!"

Anna felt her loathing toward Po quickly growing. "Try me," she muttered through clenched teeth.

For a heartbeat, she thought she saw his eyes widen, but then his face was once again impassive.

As if he was trying to hypnotize her, Po fixed his unblinking gaze on her.

"You know how dangerous it would be for you to fight

me?" he explained slowly. "Only some canlemarks ago you performed a very exhausting spell—I heard rumors of a strange ghost that saved King Raven's ship, and then I found blood on a stone here above. Your blood. You remember that one? Well, that was your biggest mistake: you saved the ship and wasted most of your energy. You saved the vessel to lose the captain." Po shook his head, clearly pitying her. "Too weak, too young, too tempered! What a waste!"

Anna knew he was right—she still felt weak after that particular spell. She wouldn't last long in a fight, but she would fight until her last breath.

Encouraging her, Raven gently squeezed her hand and whispered, "Anna, I'm with you."

Addressing Po with a disdainful smile, Anna answered, "You don't understand. The ship is salvation!"

She was not sure where it came from, she just felt it was the wise thing to say. And it worked—Po's eyes flashed with anger.

"As you wish!" he snapped, and his spell instantly hit her magical shield.

Po was a very skilled and cunning enemy. While his priests attacked her protective shield to weaken her, he attacked her mentally, trying to break into her mind and thus make her abide.

Anna yelled as a sharp, blinding pain seared through her head. Po was searching her memories. She didn't resist but concentrated on maintaining her shield, knowing that without it, they were both doomed.

Raven yelled her name, and his voice seemed to come from afar, muffled by the piercing pain. She felt him pulling his hand from hers and tried to tighten the grip, but he insisted. Something cold and hard slid between their palms. Anna felt it turn, parting their hands further. She tightened her grip, trying to get a better hold on Raven's hand. With one sharp move, the cold object was gone, and Raven's palm pressed safely against hers. It was all that mattered. She gripped him with all her might, struggling against the horrible pain in her skull.

All of a sudden, the pain stopped, and Po withdrew from her mind. Anna braced herself, her chest rising and falling rapidly. She blinked, and everything instantly came into focus. She had to try and guess Po's next move. In front of her, Po frowned, anger and disbelief written in his eyes. He did not stop. For some reason, his spell had stopped working.

And then Raven's voice echoed inside her head.

"Anna, it's me. Please, do not resist!"

Anna gasped. How could that be possible?

"I don't know. I only wanted to help you." Raven's voice answered.

"You can hear my thoughts!" Anna was delighted.

"Aye. Use my strength." Raven's hand squeezed hers, and Anna looked down.

Blood was oozing from their entwined fingers. Understanding dawned on her.

"You cut our hands! The blood connection!"

She couldn't help it—an elated laugh broke from her lips. Mesmerized, she let her mind wash into this new, wonderful connection. They had never been this close yet. They could share feelings and even see through each other's eyes! Overwhelmed with happiness, Anna wished they could remain like that forever—two in one and one in two.

Po's eyes narrowed, and he attacked again. Anna saw it coming and knew she would have no trouble resisting. When Po's spell hit her protective shield, something else happened—the shield suddenly lit up, and a ring of bright golden light formed around Anna and Raven.

"We are glowing!" Anna thought excitedly. *"How did you do it?"*

"Our own magic?" Raven offered, grinning happily.

Around them, the priests stopped in bewilderment. No one had ever seen anything like that.

An angry scowl twisted Po's neatly shaven face. He ordered the priests to continue, and their attacks were renewed, stronger than before. A rainfall of deadly spells poured down on Anna and Raven's shield from all sides.

The ring of golden light withstood the attack. Anna and Raven remained unharmed behind it. Still, they both knew that it would have to end. Together, they considered their options.

Po grinned madly and whispered something to a priest standing next to him. The latter instantly disappeared into the darkness.

Both Anna and Raven knew that nothing good would come of it. Po would never let them go.

"Together," Raven whispered.

"In life and death," Anna echoed and turned toward him.

Hand in hand, standing close together, they drew a last, deep breath. Raven raised his sword, ready to finish it in one powerful strike.

Then everything happened too fast: the priest emerged, holding a large cage. The black raven was trapped inside it. The priest screamed a spell, and the bird's piercing, pain-filled croak tore through the night. Raven's sword glittered in the golden light of their protective shield, and the worst pain ever seared through both of them. Anna's silent scream mixed with Raven's, and she felt the sword scratching her neck, and then she was falling into the darkness. She was falling too fast, limp and breathless. Raven's hand was slipping out of hers. She struggled to strengthen her grip, but her whole body was pure, blazing pain. Her fingers closed over empty air, and

for the very last time, she heard Raven's voice in her mind.
"I love you!"

Epilogue

The spell on the bird worked perfectly—the glowing ring gave way, and Po's spell pushed Raven away from Anna just in time to save her from his sword. Unspeakable! The bastard from the North thought that he had the right not only to steal, but also to kill the woman! Po's woman, his rightful reward and possession! The main priest strode toward their unconscious bodies and angrily kicked Raven.

Raven did not even groan. Both his and Anna's faces showed pain. It made Po's heart soar with satisfaction—they deserved pain, a lot of it, the more the better. Summoning the ropes to bind them, the main priest promised himself that he was going to make sure the both of them got all the pain they deserved.

"Put them alone in separate cells, and make sure they are as far from each other as possible," he ordered. Was he imagining it, or did his loyal servants exchange looks before moving the prisoners away? He decided he would deal with that later.

A young priest was waiting for them at the castle gate.

"Your Highness," he bowed, "we have caught an intruder in your room."

Forgetting about his prisoners for a moment, the main priest hurried after the youngster. Seven of his loyal servants waited for him there, guarding the intruder they had caught before his arrival.

Po's brow rose as his eyes fell over the unconscious firmly tied body that lay on the floor at his feet. He instantly recognized the tiny old woman, with her shiny golden hair.

"She was trying to steal this," one of the priests informed him, indicating the big blood-red ruby, one of Po's most treasured possessions. "She panicked and didn't even resist as we knocked her out."

"Of course," Po thought, smugly. *"She wasn't able to deal with all of my protective spells, which had informed my guards of her presence. How stupid of her, especially given that she's not that young!"* His thin lips twisted with disdain as he pushed the woman's motionless body with the tip of his shoe.

"What do you want us to do with her, Your Highness?"

"Take her to the prison and make sure she doesn't escape. Let me know when she wakes up. We have a lot to talk about."

The priest bowed respectfully and made Nim's inert body rise into the air and soar in front of him.

Po watched Nim being taken away. When the last priest disappeared, closing the door behind him, Po walked to the table and took the round ruby. A grin curled over his lips when he discovered that the woman had only touched the stone without using magic on it.

Caressing the cold surface of the mysterious ruby, the main priest felt deeply satisfied. His first victory was invigorating. The world was suddenly colorful and full of new, exciting possibilities, which made life so much more pleasant and attractive. Finally, after so many years!

"Luck is on my side …" Po whispered to the ruby, as if it were alive. "Anna, her man, and even her guardian! I have them all! *And* alive!"

Acknowledgements

I am eternally grateful to all my readers and fans for your encouragements, sweet messages and unconditional support. This book would have never been published without you guys! Philippe, Connie, Donna, ZD, Anna, Nadia, Tania, Teri, Maries, you guys are awesome! I will never be able to say this enough—Thank You!

Thank you to my wonderful editor Bronwyn for her insights and wisdom, for her constructive advice, for catching my many mistakes, and especially for her awesome ability to criticize without making me feel bad.

Many thanks to my Mom and Dad: love you to the moon and back!

Also, thank you to Yu. Even though you don't care about all my writing, you are always here for me, ready to help and endure even the most boring activities (from your point of view, lol).

And finally, thank YOU for reading my book. It means a lot to me ;-)

Please, don't be a silent reader! I'd love to hear what you think. You can reach me through my website www.katerynakei.com, on Facebook or Goodreads, or even on Amazon.

Wishing you all the very best,

Kateryna Kei

© Kateryna Kei, 2013, 2019
Dépôt légal mars 2020
Edité par KEI Inc
4 rue Raoul Busquet 13006 Marseille

www.ingramcontent.com/pod-product-compliance
Lightning Source LLC
LaVergne TN
LVHW041707060526
838201LV00043B/609